Fiction   Robbins, Susan Pepper.
   R   One way home / Susan Pepper Robbins. -- New
           York : Random House, c1992.

            175 p.

            ISBN 0-679-41404-5(alk. paper) : $16.50

            I. Title.

   3746   92-50508

ONE
Way
Home

ONE
Way
≋ *Home*

SUSAN PEPPER ROBBINS

Random House
New York

Copyright © 1993 by SUSAN PEPPER ROBBINS

All rights reserved under International and Pan-American Copyright
Convention. Published in the United States by Random House, Inc.,
New York, and simultaneously in Canada by Random House
of Canada Limited, Toronto.

Library of Congress Cataloging-in-Publication Data
Robbins, Susan Pepper.
One way home / Susan Pepper Robbins.
p. cm.
ISBN 0-679-41404-5 (alk. paper)
I. Title.
PS3568.02325R58 1992
813'.54—dc20   92-50508

Manufactured in the United States of America on acid-free paper

23456789

First Edition

Book design by Collin Leech

To my mother,
and to
Roy, Ben, and Meade

Acknowledgments

I am grateful to Stanley Beitler, editor and publisher of Independence Publishers, Inc., Atlanta, Georgia, for his idea that I expand my short story "River and Jungle" into a novel and for his early support for my work. The first chapter was published in the *Carolina Quarterly* as a story. Hampden-Sydney College provided financial support for the revision of the novel and Professors Hassell Simpson and James Schiffer encouraged me greatly. Thanks are due to Peggy Baggett of the Virginia Commission for the Arts, Carol Hoover of Ariadne Press, and to the members of the Staunton Writers Group, Margaret and Fletcher Collins, Janet Lemke, and Katie Letcher Lyle. I appreciate my family and friends, especially my brother, W. E. Pepper, and his family, and those who read and talked to me about the manuscript at various stages and so generously lent me their energy, sympathy, and insight: Maria Baber, Atalissa Sparks Gilfoyle, Frieda Baker, Bobbie and George Robbins, Betty Bebout, Catherine and Forrest Taylor, Cathy Cox, Bonnie and Bob Robbins, Mary Grattan, Carolyn Baber, Grace Simpson, Margaret and Louis Mortimer, Julie Rea, Diana Westbrook, Lynn Graham-Smith, Rosalind Hingeley, Amanda Meers, Rebecca Owen, Lindsay Nolting, Jean

ACKNOWLEDGMENTS

Saucer, Sally Doud, Phil Phelps, Jane Holland, Jamie and Homer Waits, Ken Jones, Wendy Bailey, Marilyn and Sasha Scott, Evelyn Pulley, and Kathy Leutze. I owe thanks to Carol Bly, Mary Morris, Becky Saletan, and Jennifer Ash. To J. Pendleton Baber, Ellen Levine, and Ken Norwick, I will always be grateful.

ONE
Way
Home

J know I have to stop sleeping with my sons. I switch off, the twelve-year-old one night, the eight-year-old the next. Not every night, just the nights I can't sleep. They sleep like rocks in a canyon, so I don't worry about any Oedipal business, but it would be embarrassing at school if Richie should slip and say, "Last night when I rolled over, I kicked Mama . . ." or something like that.

Being four years older than Andrew, a whole generation of childhood, Richie would say it if he thought of it. Anything to get the attention of his teachers. He's impressed them with his drug pusher handshake. He can do the smoker's last cough, the recovering alkie's cracked smugness. "Hello, I'm Richie and I'm an alcoholic," he says. He calls them his adult comedy routines. He is working up the abused child act because he knows all the drama that "goes down" when a kid in his class is pale, bruised, withdrawn, and stutters, and the principal calls in Social Services.

I tell him he could stand some withdrawal, some bruises. He laughs and pats my head as if he were calming down a new puppy and says to me, "Now, Ruth, now, Ruth."

No, we don't have a dog. Andrew wants one and acts like one at the mall to shame me. I have learned my lesson about mixing dogs and single parenting. We had a wolfhound we called Alexi; last year we chose him from the pre-gas cages at the Society for the Prevention of Cruelty to Animals. As soon as we got him home—at that point we were in a second-story apartment over in Southside—Alexi got himself run over, and I mean Run Over. Jeep Eagles don't graze, they crush. I don't want to go through that again—dog bleeding, child crying, dog bleeding, child vomiting.

If I get another dog, Andrew will pass third grade, he says. Last year it was a bike, I remind him. But it broke, he says. Forget it, I tell him.

Andrew likes for me to be called in for conferences with his teachers. He likes to go too and offer his opinions about his lack of attention in class or his troubles being the new kid in class. At those sessions he's all ears and keeps his eyes on the teacher's face.

It's not unusual for the teachers to edge up to the subject of "your life-style" after Andrew finishes with them. They carefully ask how often Andrew gets to be with his father, or if I have considered the stability a pet, maybe a dog, would offer him. These conferences kill me; my insides roll across America and I know it's time to start to think about moving again.

After the last conference I say, "Go live with your dad and get yourself twenty dogs." I turn to Richie to keep things even. "You and your brother go, and you won't have to act abused." Richie thinks I'm funny and laughs his Alzheimer's laugh, a bark and pause, a sigh and pause, which I remind him he learned from going to work with me. He says what he always says, about his dad not being able to hurt a flea. He can't figure out what scares me. I can't explain it clearly enough, just a freezing around my eyes and shooting chills down through my bones. I have sense enough to know that what I feel is some ancient instinct, or maybe I've inherited my mother's sixth sense about what to worry about. On my own I've learned when enough is enough, when to leave.

Sometimes I wish Richie had told the not-hurting-a-flea business to the teacher two moves back who nosed up to me and asked if we had ever been abused. She asked about "violent episodes" and murmured "spouse abuse." I thought she was saying "house rescue," so I an-

swered that we always lived in apartments. She looked at me funny
and got me some coffee from the teachers' lounge.

I have tried to explain to Richie that hurting or not hurting fleas is
not the thing that is wrong with his father. I have gone into the why's
of the divorce with him, but he just shakes his head as if I weren't
making sense. When I give examples, concrete ones, of the differ-
ences between his father's nature and mine, of how I have seen the
light about grown-up life and Big Rich who prefers not to grow up,
and all that split us up—not that I can go into the specifics yet; I'll
have to wait until Richie has had his own heart broken, run over by
a Jeep Eagle—then he laughs a laugh that gives me the shivers, it
sounds so old. I can't tell them all there is to know. I don't have it all
straight myself yet. There was what happened, and there was why
what happened happened—and neither the what nor the why is easy
to explain. I wish now that I had not named Richie after his father.

When I was growing up, my family, when we were at our best,
signed our dogs' names to birthday cards, all mixed in with the
people's names. We sent presents to pets on special occasions too.
Loving dogs and worrying ourselves to death about one another—I
mean, Mama about Daddy, not him about her—took the place religion takes in some families, I think. Mama had a holy place in her
heart where she worried about Daddy and me. My brother, James,
didn't need as much worrying about. I think I inherited her religion
of worrying about other people, of feeling their deepest needs. My
mistake has been thinking I knew exactly how to fix things up for
them.

So I do know how much Andrew wants a dog, but that's not my
point right now. I have to think about my life in little compartments—
Mama and Daddy in one, Rich and our married life in another, Richie
and Andrew in another, my career in old people's homes in another.
I can think about all these things one at a time but not all at once.

"Big Rich and I got a divorce because we have different natures."
That's not the whole story by a long shot, not even the tip of the
iceberg.

"I can't write that down in my social studies report on divorce,"
Richie told me last year, "and I can't write about signing pet names!"
It was one of the few times I've seen him cry since he was four years

old. Later, I found out that he wrote on some form new students have to fill out that I was an "early-stage alcoholic." A social worker came by to ask if I wanted to try Group.

I try a larger example: "Your father sees this life as one of many 'options' he has, or will have. I see this life as the one and only. We have to make a go of what we have right now."

"So?"

"He thinks a person can live anywhere, do anything, because it doesn't really matter. I think we are what we are and must do just one thing. And we get to do it once."

"That's a good combination! Two opposites, what's wrong with that? It works for other parents," Richie yells.

I'm yelling too at this point, something I have tried and tried to stop doing, but I want him to hear a story that will show him what I can't explain, I hope.

"Did you know Big Rich lived in Colombia, the country in South America?" I scream.

"I don't know if I knew that or not." He's screaming too and I bet the downstairs neighbors are listening.

"Well, he did. Now listen carefully, and maybe you'll understand the big difference between your father and your mother." I calm down, hearing the good intentions in my voice. "He lived there for a little while with a family who had two sons. One day Chichi suggested they go upriver to check on the cattle herd. Chichi was the hot-blooded one, and Evaldo was just like your dad. The brothers and Big Rich packed the boat and paddled all day to a mud bank in the middle of the jungle. They pulled the boat up and walked five miles in the dark to an Indian hut, where they sat around a fire eating chicken and drinking a homemade drink that soon had Chichi mad as fire about something political. He pulled out his gun and was going to kill the Indian and his own brother and your father and probably the Indian woman who had cooked the chicken. For some reason, he didn't. But he did something almost as bad: he staggered out of the hut, drunk, back to the river, took the boat and went home. Evaldo and Big Rich, two of a kind, slept all night, glad to be alive, and the next day began the three-day walk through the jungle to home."

Richie looks at me as if I were the one who couldn't understand the story. "So?" He shrugs. "River or jungle. Two ways home."

I can't help crying, "But it didn't then, and doesn't now, upset Big Rich what could have happened in the hut, in the jungle on the way home, or on the river going up to the middle of the jungle. The snakes in the jungle, the gun in the hut in the middle of nowhere, the piranha in the river, and him, a high school basketball star from North Carolina! Can't you see all that?"

"No, I can't, I guess," says my honor-roll, 110-pound, five-foot-seven twelve-year-old.

"Me neither," says his loyal brother. "I like the hot-blooded one with the gun. The one who took the boat and went home in the dark."

I give up again on helping them understand our lives.

"Pray for a dog," I say. They've never heard this part of the story. "Yes," I go on in a soft, televangelist voice, "I prayed for a dog when I was eight years old. I got two cocker spaniels, so the next year, I picked out a horse, not the actual horse, but the color I wanted, and this you won't believe, but I got a horse!" By now the boys are drinking in every word. I am fired up by the truth of what I'm telling them.

"I made a deal with the Lord: I would kneel down, no matter where, and pray. It was the no-matter-where business that must have gotten His attention because after a few public kneelings, I had two dogs and began working on the horse."

Andrew begs for more.

"Oh yes, her name was Beauty, and yes, she was also black, but in the winter her coat turned a reddish color that was just as beautiful. In the summers, I used to tie her to the clothesline and scrub her with Breck shampoo. She looked like a big mountain of whipped cream with a black head. When I rinsed her with ice cold water, she whinnied and danced, nuzzling me until I was covered with water and soapsuds too. The hose ran directly from the pump at the well; the water came from the middle of the earth. We were famous for our water, the taste of it. Beauty would put her head down and let me get her mane and then believe it or not, she would lie down on her side so I could soap up her stomach. She was a Morgan and lived to be twenty-seven years old. She died of old age."

"Could she gallop?" Andrew always asks, knowing I'll start on the wheelbarrow story.

They know all about Beauty and the little farm where I grew up, the well water, the apple-nut-raisin cakes with brown sugar icing Mama made every Saturday. It's a Disney world to them, and more and more to me, too. I'm losing little by little, I think, the bad part, the part I can't tell them about, the sense of being lost in a place where I knew every tree and creek by heart.

I begin the story Andrew wants to hear for the millionth time. I will do anything for him when he looks at me the way he looks at his teachers in the conferences. His eyes are gray-green, ocean color, and can be rough seas or flat. I have made him apple-nut-raisin cupcakes in the middle of the night when he asked me, acting as if we were at a teacher conference instead of in the dark in a new apartment with half-unpacked suitcases.

"Once, we got up to a gallop, but for some unknown reason she stopped mid-gallop, and I went flying over her head and landed on the ground, which was hard as concrete. We hadn't had rain for five weeks. 'Help, I'm dying,' I yelled to the sky. Pretty soon, my daddy, your grandad, came up and asked me what was wrong. 'I'm dying from broken bones,' I said. He turned and walked slowly to the shed and got the wheelbarrow, rolled it up to me, and said, 'Get in.' "

This "Get in" of my dad's kills the boys. They like me to end the story right there and not explain that I was so mad I got up and walked to the house.

"What about the dogs?" Richie asks.

"Two cockers, one rusty and one blond. Sweet as sugar."

Richie always wants me to invite a teacher home with him for supper. "Just fix a pizza," he says.

"What am I supposed to do with a teacher?" I ask him.

"Act natural"—he laughs—"or talk big. Anything. Teachers like to hear talking of any kind so they can talk back. Get them going and you have it made."

Andrew agrees with every word his brother says about dogs and teachers. He adds "Just pizza" and "Act natural" in rap music rhythms to what Richie is saying.

Richie makes it his business to be the teacher's pet every year, no matter how terrible the new teacher is. He brings home notes about his potential and what a pleasure or joy he is in social studies.

Andrew approaches teachers in a different way. He becomes their problem. He has never brought home a good note, just ones setting up the conferences he loves. Richie drags me to all the PTO meetings, especially the ones where we sit in student desks and try to answer questions. He coaches me before we go so I can do well in the miniclasses and in the conferences. "Say," he tells me, " 'Richie has always loved learning.' Say, 'Richie enjoys the challenge of your assignments.' "

Andrew just looks at us practicing for Parents' Night. "Can I have a dog?" he asks patiently, his eyes a flat seawater green-gray.

When I got home on Tuesday—at this point the three of us are in another second-story place in Richmond's Northside—I should have known something was going on by the way the hall rugs were sloshed up against the baseboards. In fact, it looked as if Andrew might have found himself the twenty dogs I had mentioned and brought them home to feed.

The boys show signs of being river-jungle types: live with me, live with Big Rich. Either way, they are living, having a home, getting through childhood, which is a drag, Richie tells me. I want them with me, period. Big Rich thinks it's okay to have a wife or an ex-wife, for him to live with me or live near me, either one is living. It's okay, he thinks, to have the boys with him or with me, if he's near them.

I'm an administrative aide in charge of activities at Elder Home—they all call me Ruth Activities. I take the boys to work when I can get by with it. They're helping stack linens, I tell my supervisor, Mrs. Osborne, who thinks kids are as bad as old people.

Once when we were living in Petersburg—we have worked our way up from North Carolina, and will probably end up in Maine before the boys finish high school—I came home to find Richie had stashed his dad in the closet. The hall rugs were washed up against the baseboards that day, too. Big Rich goes along with the idea that kids need a father's presence, but he likes to be needed in splashes, like paint thrown on a wall. It's vivid all right when he appears, but then I make him leave. I divorced him when Andrew was two; I mean I tried to divorce him. He refuses to be divorced and won't do anything terrible enough to get a court order with teeth in it against him. The letters from judges he makes into paper airplanes and sends to us. He follows us, but I keep moving or having the locks changed. The boys see it as a game. Six years is a long time to play a game.

This "divorce" is unusual. I think it is, anyway. I am on the run from Richie and Andrew's dad. Most of the time, I read, it's the dad who wants to put distance between himself and his ex. Not Big Rich. I can never reenter the singles scene because I'll never be single again.

He can't work, he says, because of our divorce. I never give him time to establish credit or build up a relationship with employers because I'm always moving.

"I'm moving, yes, I'm moving," I yell, "because you are following."

I have a career in long-term care for the elderly, so I can work anywhere, any time. Old people are all over. I know in my heart this is the work I was meant to do. I get us settled in a place, and bingo, I'm at work.

There's never been a problem finding a job. When the newest Ms. Whoever asks me across her desk in my interview about my frequent moves, I first try the up-front approach, straight from the shoulder and the heart, something like, "I have an unresolved divorce situation." Then comes the follow-up question I'm getting used to: "What are you afraid of?" I can see Ms. Whoever thinking she has a battered woman on her hands, a real nutcase who will bring trouble into her old people's lives and her nice office. She thinks some violent and crazed ex will be hanging around me and ruining the atmosphere she's creating of sharing and concern. But her problem is she can't look as if she didn't sympathize with a battered woman on the run, much as she does not want to hire one. I assure her that violence is not in the picture, but that the situation is complicated. Which God knows it is. Reassured, she hires me on the spot. Burnout is a career hazard for Activities people and there's always an opening.

Richie is like me in the way he can fit in at any new school. He fits in no matter what kind of school it is—old-fashioned, with tracked classes for the college-bound smart rich kids; or mainstreamed classes of kids of all colors and incomes, the mix-'em-up-we're-here-to-enjoy-learning schools. Andrew has adjustment problems at every new school, according to the counselors. I think it's his genes. He's Big Rich all over again. He's doing exactly what he wants to. "Following his own agenda," according to his latest counselor; not the school's, not mine, just his own.

Tuesday, the hamburger I planned for supper was gone, and the white Styrofoam tray with the tatters of Saran Wrap was stuck down in the garbage can by the sink. It looked as if Andrew had fed a whole package of ground beef, extra lean, to the dog.

What dog?

See how my thinking is controlled by my children: there was no dog, was not going to be a dog, in our little setup. I have said a million times to the boys, "We do not live on a farm, which is a place dogs like. We are apartment people."

But when I saw that the hamburger was gone, I began thinking automatically, well, the dog must have eaten my hamburger.

I could see the hamburger had not been cooked. No dirty pans. No smoke hanging in a greasy cloud in a corner of the kitchen, no ketchup bottle on the table. The boys had not been cooking. Big Rich had not dropped by and fixed them his special bacon cheeseburgers.

Sometimes I know Big Rich has gotten into the kitchen and been cooking with the boys while I'm at work. There are signs of a feast, even though the kitchen is cleaner than when I cook. The boys are full, for one thing, and won't look at what I fix them. They let him in when he finds us. They have themselves big reunions while I'm working. It makes me mad, but what can I do? I deal with the problem by moving.

Richie knows "all the literature" on latchkey children from his counselor at school and goes on with his life while I'm at work. He tries out new recipes, calls his dad long-distance when he can find him and tells him where we are, has friends over, whatever. So far, he has not had a teacher over, as far as I can tell, much as he wants to.

Richie respectfully refuses to help his brother with his math and reading. "Andrew has learning disabilities, probably emotional ones, which at this point I am not equipped to deal with." He laughs. Andrew says, "Uh-huh, that's true, Mom," and adds, "If I had a dog, I could learn nine times eight and read at grade level."

In case of trouble Richie is prepared to call the 911 numbers to get the "proper authorities in on the situation." He has passed down to Andrew like old clothes the basics of living the latchkey life: fires, strangers, doctors.

I sneak down the hallway to the closet door and whoosh it open, expecting Big Rich to fall out, either playing dead or grabbing at me as if he were dying.

I feel sometimes that we will never really divorce—I mean actually *be* divorced. It's fate, but I'm lucky, as I said, in my work, and can keep on the move. Second-story apartments are my forté. I can get us going in no time. Once we lasted seven months in one place, it was in High Point, without Big Rich's finding us, which was almost a whole school year. Richie was on the honor roll and Andrew made straight N's—Needs Improvement, his best set of grades yet.

Nothing, not a body or an ex-husband, falls out, so I slam the door, almost disappointed. There must be something else going on. My nose is really twanging now.

We're second-floor this time in a big old house with a slate roof that has a geography of its own, hills, peaks, crevasses, slopes, plains. There are overhangs and places to hide. The landlord has warned me not to let the kids play on the roof.

"One child fell to her death," he said slowly, then added, "Parts have rotten beams under them, but worse, slate cracks. Only experts or animals can walk on slate."

Why did he mention animals, we wondered, understanding that expert roofers could learn to walk like Indians distributing their weight noiselessly through their feet.

Our long windows look out into other windows, so you can see into other rooms, getting scraps of sky and trees as you look. I always try to find an unusual place for us; it's the least I can do as a single parent.

Richie points out that often he has two parents, with Big Rich showing up in closets and parked vans so often. "Not two moneywise and quality-time-wise," I say, and that shuts him up.

I shriek for Andrew. No answer. I yell, "I know there's a dog there, a wet one who ran down the hall."

Andrew sticks his head around his bedroom door. "Dog? I wish I had seen one. Did you bring me one? If you did, I'll pass third grade."

He's starting to cry when I say, "Forget it."

He looks at me in the teacher way. "Can we have fish sticks tonight with apple cupcakes?"

"I planned Texasburgers, but someone stole the hamburger."

"Must be some wild dog," he says, calm again.

"There are no wild dogs loose in the city," I explain, sniffing the air. I start the oven for the frozen fish sticks. "Where's my little pan I use in the oven?" He doesn't know. Richie is at school practicing for the play about drugs he helped write; he got the lead. He "opens," he calls it, Halloween night, a Friday.

We eat the fish sticks with straight lines of ketchup on them, and a can of biscuits. I peel apples for the cupcakes. While they are baking, I lie down to begin a night of television and wine. First I yell at Andrew's door, "Do your homework." It's a good night on twelve—*Highway to Heaven* and a special on the homeless. I look for Big Rich's face when they do close-ups of the men, who all look like Willie Nelson.

Something scrapes and a draft of wet air blows in from under Richie and Andrew's door right at my feet.

"Did you open the window?" I yell.

"Just to see if it's still raining," he calls back. "I'm shutting it now." There's a bang.

"I thought I heard a dog," I yell.

"No such luck," he yells back. Then he adds in a sweeter yell, "Want to help me with my multiplication?" This is a first.

"In a minute," I yell, surprised and a little mad at having to do homework.

I must have been sleeping, dreaming halfway, but I swear I heard a conference going on. Richie had come home. He was telling his dad that it would be no problem to keep the dog on the roof.

Then I thought I heard Andrew saying, "You could too, Dad. Come in through our window when you need anything." There was more talk of blankets and tents and food. I decided I was dreaming and went into real sleep until morning.

I sidle along the walls, making my way to the kitchen, smelling the grease and ready to pounce on the frying pan, but as the boys come into view, innocent over their cereal bowls, in T-shirts and underpants, no frying pan anywhere, I think the terrible thought that has often split my head open: I am losing my marbles.

I straighten up. Forget it, just let's forget it. Then I feel much better. I'll start my life over this morning. Nobody but me and two boys here. No dog on the roof, no ex-husband, less wine sloshing around in my head from now on. I'm saying all this more or less out loud as I sail into the kitchen.

"Good morning," Richie and Andrew almost chime, but their heads are low over the bowls, so I can't see their faces, the blurry secrets they keep from me written on their perfect cheeks and down their perfect noses. Rich's high bridge and my ski slope haven't asserted their genetic powers yet.

I shake my head; the new perm lets off a nice, astringent, new kind of smell and the new color is autumn haze. I like having a cloud of hair, a pale cloud. Very nice. Very different from the long smooth braid I used to wear. Like all the women I see, the older I get, the younger I wear my hair.

Forget the dog on the roof, drop it. It was a dream. Let sleeping dogs lie. Okay, "sleeping dogs" is not a good way to think about forgetting things I need to forget, like dogs, to get through today. Forget the grease smell. I must have dreamed it.

It's Friday. In twenty-five minutes I will have to be at work, early, to hide the "medications" Mrs. Osborne "administers" to the old people to keep them out of her hair. We're expecting a "surprise" tomorrow, a state inspection. It could mean the end of Mrs. Osborne.

If Louise McFarland comes walking at a slant down the hall, her lips dry and cracked, her eyes set in gelatin from Mrs. Osborne's dosing her up on Mellaril, the state inspector will shut the place down. Or should.

"Nothing will happen, believe me. I have the inspector's old aunt on my waiting list. Count on it, he'll see our strong points. Elder Home will get a good report." This was last week when Mrs. Osborne was tying one of the old zombies in her chair and propping one on the couch in front of the big-screen TV. Then she stood up and watched Louise McFarland slanting down the hall, hands out in front of her, looking for a railing or cane or somebody to grab on to.

Some days Elder Home is a drug colony. I'd like to see Mrs. Osborne fired, busted for pushing drugs, but it's less trouble to go along with everything, for this Saturday inspection anyway.

Anyway, I'd probably get the ax, not Mrs. O.

"Did you put away the medications?" she asks me, in a voice that lets me know I'm in on the deal same as she is. She knows I will hide the pills for her. We sound like a vice squad on the take, blackmailing each other into loyalties. It's as if we were married in that way.

She knows I have just signed up for benefits at Elder Home, so I won't run any risks with my job. Crazy Ozone Layer, that's my nickname for Mrs. Osborne, expects the drugs to disappear, and they do when I'm around. Magic.

Ozone Layer is full of stupid ideas for me to do for Activities. She doesn't know that a person, especially an ancient person, cannot wave, does not want to wave scarves in an "autumn dance." Ozone Layer wants a scarf dance done from wheelchairs while her favorite records, "September Morn," "Ebb Tide," and "Theme from Tara," play. Her ideas of geriatric fun do not suit the group of people we have at Elder Home.

Last Thursday, sitting in a circle and waving our scarves to the music, like dried-up little E.T.'s, we scarf-danced the afternoon away.

It will take me three hours to walk the Mellaril out of the zonked ones—Louise and Bonnie and Horace, the ones who've had the most popped into them. Bonnie's girlfriend is Edith, who is a young eighty-two, but whose arms are the color of old bricks because the skin is dissolving under the glassy skin tape, "second skin," it's called, with good reason. "Too much pregnant-zone," she explains, meaning prednisone, holding out her arms as if she were a teenager showing off her tan.

I'm no shining example of the drug-free life with my swollen, bruised wino head, but I am all they've got to lean on.

"Today, I'm at Elder Home until six to get ready for a big inspection. You two go to soccer practice after school. Money is here by the phone for lunch. You walk, I'll drive. Any questions?"

They catch the new-day upswing in my voice and jump in. Richie reaches for me and talks through a milky kiss.

"There's a letter for you from the teacher under my books on the floor. I was supposed to give it to you last week, but then I lost it for a while. Now, though, it's here. See. I'll microwave you a cup of coffee while you read it. You have time. Mrs. Ozone Layer can rot. There are some more letters here too. I forgot."

We move piles of papers, undone, half-done homework, looking for letters he remembers seeing somewhere, someplace. How many letters have come and stayed in a pile and gotten thrown away un-opened, unseen by me. I have tried to teach them to recognize my mother's backward left-handed writing so they will save hers, but I can tell that many of her letters have been lost from the tone in the next one I get: "Ruth, I know you can do anything, but do be careful" crackles up from the airmail envelopes she uses as if she were an ocean away instead of with my brother in Illinois.

I know I talk too much about my work and boss around the boys. I know I yell too much about lost letters. Richie yells back that I only write to one person, Grammer in Illinois, so what's the big deal since she writes to us whether we write or not. I get off the subject of lost letters.

17

"Mrs. O. has her good side," I begin. "Look, we have benefits, all kinds of health insurance now. You can get sick now, or have an operation if you want to."

"Right, Mom," Andrew sighs into his frosted flakes. Then he adds his favorite comeback, "I'm fine." Most of the time, Andrew's conversation doesn't connect with what I've said, but it seems to now.

I find the teacher's letter. It's dirty and damp, but I have my cup of coffee and it's a letter, anyway. I feel much better, civilized, even. Mom is reading a letter from the teacher over coffee. The kids are eating a wholesome breakfast—there's milk in the cereal today; sometimes they eat it dry or with orange juice or Coke—before a day of school and soccer practice. And somewhere in the apartment there's a letter from my children's grandmother.

Richie puts two aspirin by the coffee cup. He has washed the wineglass I left by the couch last night.

Ms. Vincent has used a form letter to parents. My name is written in on a long blank. Richie's name is written in on the blank down in the paragraph about the policy of the school on conferences and individual attention. Would I fill in the blanks below, Ms. Vincent wants to know, telling her alternate times in my late-afternoon schedule so she can fit me in with the other parents. The letter does not hint at what the problem is.

I thought Richie was problem-free. It's Andrew who has school problems, isn't it?

I wish I could go for a conference about myself: individualized motherhood instruction. I yell at Richie as he's leaving. What have you done? I thought you loved school. He yells back through the door that he does, but he failed the drug test.

I knock over the coffee when I run to grab him. What test, what drugs? The hall is slanting like the *Titanic*. I'm a Mellaril junkie, a Darvon doll baby, a wino. We're sinking through to the first floor. I have Richie's collar in my fist.

"Mom"—the now-now voice, the I've-got-to-be-careful-with-the-crazy-here voice. "We had a stupid little drug test, not a blood test, just a checklist thing, and I missed enough to be in the high-risk category. It's nothing. I had a too-big hole in my jeans, I forgot my homework twice in a row, and I fell asleep in social studies. That's what qualified me. All you have to do is go have the conference, say

I'm not a problem, not a bed wetter with a chronic nose drip, a danger to society or myself, and I'm back in business again. It was just a new drug checklist that some guy, some expert, came to give the whole school. I asked him if he'd go over to Elder Home to give a slide show for your goldie-oldies. I thought they would like to hear about kids and drugs. Old people like to hear about kids on drugs, statistics about teen suicide, all that about how terrible everything is today."

He runs for the door, telling me to choose three times to go see Ms. Vincent and something else about this specialist in drugs coming to see me at Elder Home next week some afternoon, and can I come to school soon to get stuff straight.

Again, next morning, same thing. I am sneaking to the kitchen, bent over and wrapped in a gold thermal blanket beaded with polyfiber balls. Here I am, spying on my children, again, who are fixing their own breakfast, again. Things seem tilted and about to spill.

Andrew is saying through the crunch and milk of frosted flakes, "Mom wants us to be happy. She always says that. We don't have to tell her. Grammer in Illinois wants us all to be happy. Look at what she doesn't know anyway."

Richie is frying an egg, rolling the pan to get the grease to run over the yolk, sunny-side. "It'd be better to have an older one, or one that was trained, sort of, that was quiet and would do what we wanted plus understand how we live, about Dad and everything. Like van life."

I cannot believe that they are calmly plotting to get a dog, an old quiet one, who would live somewhere out of my sight and, in his doggy brain, understand our family. I cannot believe I'm understanding my family as a dog would, by listening and watching every move.

What does a person do in the split second before she goes around the bend? That instant when it's clear that the car is out of control?

I burst into the kitchen like a yellow bat, my new hazy hair standing twelve inches up and around my head.

"What do you mean, 'old and quiet' and 'fitting in'? Didn't I explain how a dog cannot come here? We cannot have a dog."

Richie turns, holding the pan up off the burner. "We're not talking about dogs." He laughs. "It's a date. For you. We are planning a date for you. We know just the person you'd like, he's just your type. Not at all like Dad. He's a regular, normal-type person. I mean he's gone to college—four years—has a job. He wears a tie. The guy I told you about yesterday. The one who's coming to Elder Home to talk about sex and drugs."

Then he goes on tilting the pan slowly and glazing his egg like an old-fashioned short-order cook in a diner. There's just one person who could have taught him that. Rich.

When Richie sees I'm staring at him slopping the hot grease over the yolks, perfectly, he stops and tries to be awkward, like a normal kid, one who doesn't know how to cook.

"You think I'm the kind of person, the kind of woman, who is just starting her thirties, who has to have an old thing around, is that what you think, that I want an old, trained boyfriend, a man in a tie, with a college degree in his hand? Get Ms. Vincent a date! She's got a college degree and may be a single person for all I know. Maybe even with no kids. I don't need you to plan talks, not ones on sex and drugs, anyway, for me at Elder Home. I am Ruth Activities, remember."

"Calm down, Mama. Get it together. We just want you to have some fun and we've found the right guy, I mean person. He acts right, he has to because it's his job. He's the drug expert I told you about. He wants to come give a slide show at Elder Home for you. He's got one called 'Dangerous Drugs,' that's the one I've seen, and he's got another, very different kind of one, on stars, the ones in the sky, not the ones in movies, he can give."

Andrew is pleased with his brother's explanation. He says he agrees that I need more fun, that having an expert around would be a help. He likes the way this man dresses. Like he's undercover. He says it was fun to fail the drug checklist. It's news to me that he had failed the drug test too.

"I do not like experts, especially ones who test my sons for drugs and fail them, and I hate having fun." It is terrible to hear myself say that, but the boys don't seem surprised.

"This person is not fun, not the way *you* think of as fun. He's fun the way you think crime shows on TV are fun." Richie thinks he's explained everything perfectly.

It is true I love crime shows and old *Highway to Heavens*—very satisfying to single mothers. Justice is done presto. Bodies jiggle from machine guns blasting away or a miracle pops up. Maybe this guy is fun in that way.

"We think you'd like Douglas. His whole name is Douglas P. Smathers. He is young, I mean your age, but he acts old, but in the good way, quiet and pleased to see things—like leaves blowing on the sidewalks. His motto, he says, is that everything is special. He's a nut about stars. He goes to the Star Gazers."

"You know how I hate the word 'special' and you know I have just started taking an interest in stars. It's nothing special. I've been to only one meeting. See, now you've got me saying 'special.' Only I mean it in a bad way. Star Gazers, stars, skies, the whole bit, I can take or leave. Stars, they are just a little hobby. I can take up birds or aerobics, whatever."

"Good, then you'll go." Andrew sticks his thumbs up, but so I won't notice, he thinks.

"When have you talked to him? Who says I'm going out with any Douglas Whatever Smathers, and I would appreciate it if you and Andrew kept out of my private life. I do not go on dates."

Andrew is getting upset at this point and slips. "Dad said it was okay for you to go out."

I'm blowing my top at seven-fifteen on Saturday morning.

"Have you been consulting Rich about this date setup too?"

Richie seems ready to murder Andrew the minute he can get rid of me.

"Look, Mom, it's time for us to leave—special Saturday-morning practice. I need fifteen dollars for the new shirts. If you will just meet Douglas Smathers after work one afternoon and talk to him about the slide show which I have already invited him to give for you. I'm sorry, I thought you needed activities for your old people. Better ones than Ozone Layer cooks up, like the scarf deal. You don't have to have a date-date, or even go out for supper, but if you'll just talk to Doug and let him show his slides, I'll help Andrew with his math. It will help us at school to get in good with Douglas Smathers. Everybody likes him, but I was the only one who could offer him old people, yours at Elder Home—an audience to listen to him."

"It's true, Mom," Andrew says, desperate to get on the good side of Richie. "Everybody wants to be around Douglas Smathers, but we were the only ones who could think of a way to catch him."

If it had not been so late—I had to go in for the Saturday "surprise" inspection—if I hadn't had a check to write for the soccer shirts, if I weren't still burning from the last visit to Andrew's teacher, who asked me point-blank if there was a lot of loud talk in my home—Andrew, it seems, would only talk at the top of his voice during class—I would not have agreed.

There is something sickening about my children fixing me up with a date, but more sickening is the suspicion that they are not sincere. That they are planning with their father, for God's sake, to marry me off to this stranger. Maybe not marry, but get me to going out on "dates" so I'd be gone a lot and they could go on with their lives, cooking meals, playing with dogs who slept on the roof.

But forget Rich for a minute, which I try to do for longer and longer stretches and am up to ninety minutes now, not counting sleeping. This whole date thing is sickening, even though I can understand it: Andrew and Richie will do anything to be popular; they get that bad trait from both parents. Now they have this cockeyed plan to get me to go out with anyone who turns up. Probably they'll give reports on our "dates" in social studies, the way they have on divorce.

Me out of the way on a date, Rich could call and talk to the boys from the phone booth two blocks away for thirty minutes without my yelling about baths or homework. Then Rich could step in from his mobile home (the van), cook supper, and go on teaching Richie how to cook.

He'd be giving quality time to his parenting and I could give the quantity time. It'll work, he is thinking. I know. River or jungle, her place or mine, her apartment or my van, so what, either way, both are good. They are my sons. They are her sons. River sons. Jungle sons. Both are good ways to be sons.

Maybe I could run off with this expert on stars or drugs and help him with his undercover work. Maybe we, the four of us, could tour American schools and be popular, give talks at assemblies, I don't know what else.

Of course, it may be that Rich and the boys have already planned for me to be thinking this way. They stay two steps ahead of me, look over their shoulders to see if I'm doing what they have in mind. Only this time I'm ahead of them. I'm planning to elope, the boys and me, with this stargazer, drug expert, undercover man.

I can feel there is more, much more, to this date thing than a simple evening out for Mom. Maybe Andrew is into a little drug deal, maybe he really has failed this drug test, is experimenting, as the television says kids do, and before you know it . . . too late, they need a six-week stay in a rehab program.

I know how much fun the idea of drugs can be. The old killer, anyway—stolen whiskey from Rich's father's cabinet, or Daddy's hidden vodka. A brand-new bottle in the culvert, leaves brushed up over it. Mama saying to me that I should watch out for my brother when Daddy "wasn't himself."

Maybe the date with the drug expert is really Andrew and Richie's way of letting me know that they both have troubles, more than I know about. This man in a tie probably has some very bad news to tell me, something "special" that he can tell me only in person. My sons have a dependency, have robbed the school cafeteria to pay the playground pusher, have guns, are keeping a secret drug pusher on the roof at school. Maybe Rich is starting a new career as a drug dealer, using the boys to make contacts at school for him.

At Elder Home, as I check on the hidden meds and spiff up the residents for the inspection, I have to admit that I am tempted to have this date, for reasons beyond the fall-off-the-tightrope one of finding out that my children are headed toward a life of needles, crime, and the streets. The temptation of simplicity: of simply going along with my children's little plans, doing what they want me to, being a good mom, a cool, neat mom. I give in to this temptation a lot—put pizza on MasterCard, charge a pair of Air Jordans (Look, Mom, $99.99 on sale, down from $120.00!). Now, I will be the mom who will have A Date. I do want to be the opposite of my mother, perfect as she was in her way. I do want to be the person that the children of alcoholics hardly ever become until they are very old, or at least middle-agers with years of sessions under their belts. I want to be free to be, excuse me, but free to be, yes, me.

I haven't had anything close to a date since Big Rich, which puts it in the century when I was fourteen, when my life careened off the track with him.

We were childhood sweethearts, if that's the word for what we were, a terrible name for a terrible affliction. A disease of the nerves, like Parkinson's, that lasts through your life without killing you—you just die still having it. It lasts into, maybe, the afterlife. Mormons, I think, believe it, and maybe I do too. You can never get rid of a childhood sweetheart because it's getting rid of your own childhood, the most dangerous part of it, the most exciting, high-adventure part, when everything—even the pages of the seventh-grade history book thumbed to a soft chamois cloth, the water fountain, ah, the water fountain, the after-school practices, the field trips—is inflamed with pre-sex sex, which is the fake kind of freedom that some children, the ones like Rich and me, know about.

And worse, we were secret sweethearts. It was Phyllis and Rich who were the sweethearts everyone knew, everyone thought would grow up to marry each other. I was their daredevil friend with the long smooth braids, two for school, one French braid for special occasions.

Rich and I knew about us. Rich and Phyllis knew about themselves. It was Phyllis and I who didn't know about each other with Rich. Same old story. One boy, two girls.

Life was a spinning dazzle. Embarrassing to remember the running, hiding, lying—the old kind of fun.

"Where are you going?" "When will you come home?" Mama asked me, the same fierce notes of motherhood ringing in her voice that I can hear more often than I like in my own voice now. *"If* you come home" was what she meant. Her fury and despair added speed to our lives. Mama worried herself almost into her grave over me and Daddy. My brother, James, she never thought about, and it helped him grow up, or seems to have helped. I call being off in Illinois, working on computers, a good life, plus having an ick of a wife and two daughters on honor roll. Mucho benefits and retirement plans, I am sure. Being in Illinois with James and his little crowd is almost graveside, in my opinion, but as Mama often says in her letters, my opinion about such a nice family is not called for. Of course, what else can she feel, trapped there, her arthritis plaiting her into macramé ropes, propped up in her wheelchair. So what if it's motorized. Sometimes her letters, the ones I find, with her note "Please Forward" on the front, the ones the boys remember to put on top of the piles of newspapers and papers, do strike me in my heart. If I had a house in one place, Mama could come live with us and not be Grammer in Illinois to Andrew and Richie, but be Grammer in Wherever-We-Are. She would love doing homework; she would help them with her favorite subjects, Latin and geometry. I wish I had done more homework. I missed out on being the perfect child of an alcoholic, somehow. I don't think straight A's and marrying a nice somebody who is normal is so bad. James got to be that child.

Rich's parents had long-range plans for him: "This boy is going to be my lawyer-boy. He will come back home after a little bit of college fun and run our orchards." Apples had made them rich. "Snotty-rich" Rich used to say. His father wanted Rich to have two careers, one safety-netting the other. "Lose a crop, so? Settle some estates to make up for the crop," Mr. McFall said, adding, "An early marriage will ruin your chances." Right in front of me, as if I were deaf as a post. Of course, he was speaking of Rich's early marriage to Phyllis. He had no idea that I would be the one to ruin his son's chances.

"Who's getting married," Rich would say back.

His parents had big plans for Rich, all right. My mother had high hopes for me, in spite of the evidence of my report cards and my torn clothes. Daddy was too drunk to have plans for anybody except who was going to get him the next bottle of King Ivan vodka. Mama wanted me to have a safer life than she had. Safety was what her high hopes translated in plain English meant.

Now I see her point. Hospitalization benefits and preventative-care dental plans are huge achievements. I wish Mama could know how I have come around to her point of view on things. My letters don't do my come-around justice.

In fact, the main reason I love old people is that they are safe. Even Mrs. Russell, who bites people, is safer than the people out there who may end up married to you. Mrs. Russell always says, after she has tried to take a chunk out of your arm, "Well, it didn't kill you, did it?" She's right, you're okay, safe as a loaf of bread.

Rich's idea of raising children is to get a dog to climb a ladder and spend the night on the roof, or to get the van rolling on two wheels, with the boys riding on the high side, calm as concrete. I caught him riding with them this way once. At his best, Rich wants them to get an egg fried perfectly, sunny-side up. He wants them to have interesting childhoods and forget adulthood, as he has. He has never gotten over his childhood; he's just trying to prolong it into theirs.

I want them to survive their childhoods, and thanks to my new benefits package, they can.

Passing me in the halls at the old high school, the two-story frame firetrap, Rich used to yell out over the herds of kids, "Sooner or later."

He meant sex, which we usually had sooner, right after school. Sex started at fourteen. I can't believe it myself. But you had to be there. Rich, the wild boy who seemed to swim in sunlight and live in trees, me, the brown girl with long braids who turned toward that light.

I cannot stand for Richie to be twelve, the same age his father and I were when we went—there's no other word for it—wrong, the pre-sex period where life chooses its level of flight.

I don't see any of Rich's insanity yet in Richie.

"Get that g-d white mule down that fire escape. You got him up there, and you can get him down or be finished with school forever right now." The seventh-grade teacher—it was her first year of teaching, poor thing—was yelling at Rich through the window. It was as shocking to hear her say "g-d" as it was to see the mule's plain-eyed stare through the window.

Rich kept shrugging his shoulders. The whole class was lumped up at the window, looking down at him. He was saying up to the teacher and to us, "Sorry, I can't hear you. I don't know what happened. The mule? I found him going up the fire escape."

We all loved Rich for getting a mule up the thirty-four steps, but I was the one who ended up marrying him. I think things like the mule on the fire escape had more to do with my addiction to Rich than I can figure out, but I remember Phyllis, even calm, beautiful Phyllis, with all of us yelling and screaming, whispering, "Three more steps, Rich." She was addicted too, but in a different way and, I think now, to a different Rich. She saw a grown-up Rich who would be different. I loved him as he was. Maybe he would have been different, the lawyer–orchard owner, if it had all worked out with Phyllis. I don't know.

After the mule, I saw school as an opportunity to impress Rich. I painted words on the roof of the school. Rich and Phyllis told me what to paint. I was out on the roof of the school, a crew of one. Night, flashlight, ladder, my idea of heaven. Rich and Phyllis watching me. Mrs. Hall, the English teacher, cried when she'd see us three together. But she cried about poems in class, so I didn't mind; in fact, it was a compliment to get her going on something sad. I didn't understand that she thought we were sad. She knew, somehow, that we were ruining one another's chances to leave North Carolina, and if people didn't leave the state, she said, they were—and here she always broke down again and had to dig for her tissues—well, she couldn't think of any other way to say it, from North Carolina, a terrible fact that explained everything—all failures, all suicides, all trouble—to her, but not to anyone else.

She cried a lot, especially, I think, over Rich and Phyllis. Me? She thought I would die in a fall before I graduated. I stole her car keys, but in an easy way, so that she thought she had forgotten she had put them on the radiator and they had slipped down behind it.

"You know, Ruth, you can get attention without breaking bones. You don't have to always have a cast on for us to sign. You can study like your two friends, Richard and Phyllis."

She could see how ill-equipped I was for anything without Rich and Phyllis. At the time, Rich and Phyllis seemed big surprises dropped down to me from the sky. I have always been a fool for surprises. Pack it in tissue with some sparkly ribbon and I'd be happy to open up a nest of snakes. Being one of a threesome was my idea of perfection. Mrs. Hall could have told me Rich and Phyllis were bombs in a pretty box, and I would have happily carried it up the nearest tree, hung upside down, and opened it. The explosion would have been worth it to me then.

Richie still looks like a baby in his chin and nose. He is still just himself, not Rich yet, not me yet. I want to make his life, and Andrew's life especially, something different from the childhood I had, different from the childhood their father had.

I don't think Richie and Andrew would disagree with me if they knew all the facts: they both want nice, safe childhoods.

Another temptation to have a date with this Douglas star-drug man, besides making my children happy (a harder thing to do than anyone knows or admits), is what it would do to Mrs. Osborne. I can just see her. The old people at Elder Home love anybody who visits. They would love the visits of criminals or prostitutes.

But Mrs. Osborne is so paranoid that she would panic at the sight of my "date." Then I could say, "Oh no, this man is here to take me out to eat Chinese and talk about a slide-show activity, stars or drugs, for the residents. He just looks like an undercover agent."

After our fight on Wednesday, Ozone Layer crooked her whole hand at me, cupping the air. "Come here, come here," she meant. She closed her office door to a crack and began shaking and screaming in whispers and hisses about the meds and asking me if I intended to keep on interfering with her administration of Elder Home. When one of the aides or nurses walked by, she'd open the door and say that we were not fighting, not fighting, just discussing and getting things straight.

"I come in on Monday, every Monday, to find Louise and Bonnie and Horace completely zonked," I told her. "How we are going to get past the state inspector another time I don't know, even with the pills hidden and not written down, and me walking them on the Bataan death march Friday to sober them up, they are still in zombie land. How many aunts does he have?"

"You know, if I were you . . ." Mrs. Osborne never finishes this sentence because she knows it's enough to shut me up. As she sees it, I'm against her and her methods for keeping things orderly and quiet at Elder Home, but she knows that I always help her out on the inspection. We have what she calls "the same goals, the same goals for Elder Home." Once she hissed this at me, but when I wiped my cheek as if she had got some spit on me, she never came up in my face again.

I can see I might have to quit, and sooner than I want to, benefits package with dental prevention or not. Usually, it's Big Rich who drives me away from a place, not a work-related situation, so maybe I'm making progress.

I read about single mothers and their need to work toward a new concept of themselves, to make independent decisions, to break away from the past, as if the past were a piece of land or an iceberg that they could float away from. It's getting smaller and smaller while a new landmass appears and gets larger and larger.

Give me a break, I mean, give me some money or a good benefits deal, and I'll give you a self-concept that will knock you over. I have a picture of the new me ready to go, even to go out on a date and have some of that new kind of fun with whatever undercover drug expert Richie and Andrew want to fix me up with. I'll go when I can get the past to stay put like a piece of land I can leave behind.

But the past, my past, anyway, is more like fog, or a virus, not an iceberg, not something I can wave good-bye to. When Rich quits showing up, I'll quit moving.

In the apartment, sitting in front of a mountain of clean clothes I'm folding from the Laundromat, I feel the fog move in on me. "Folding" is not the right word. I wrap the clothes around my fist and elbow the way carpenters do their long extension cords. Then, I'm ready to wedge the clothes into drawers.

If there were some margin of money, M-O-M, I call it, in my life, I could do a lot of things. I could be the new single parent—I look like a very good copy of one now, with my big hair—if I had the M-O-M.

Needless to say, a few weeks later, under all the pressure from Richie and Andrew, backed up by the Nightmare of Elm Street, Rich, and the dream dog at the window, I will end up talking to Douglas P. Smathers on the phone and saying I would like to talk to him about coming to Elder Home with his slides on drugs or stars.

"I'll go on this stupid date" is how I put it to myself.

"*You* ou forgot the physicals, Mom. You promised you wouldn't forget. Coach says we can't play next week if we don't have our paperwork in and *straight*—that's his word, which means every form filled out and every item checked off. You did promise us you would get our physicals, and then Richie and I promised Coach Dotson that we would have everything taken care of. We are the last ones on our teams to get everything done. The money for the shirts was only one thing on the checklist. We have to have a copy of our birth certificates, the physicals that you promised you would get for us and the forms signed by the doctor, pictures of us at about this age we are now, and then we get—we were supposed to do things in order before soccer season started—the team shirts as a reward. Coach Dotson is sorry he let us have our shirts before we had our paperwork *straight*. He thought, he said, he could trust us to get everything done. We told him we thought we could trust you. I mean I said that I had always trusted you until this, and I didn't know what had happened to you. Richie said we would get it all done this week some way. You remember you promised."

"Please stop saying 'you promised.' I forgot I promised. It's that simple. I forgot about the physicals. You are supposed to help me remember things, especially your stuff. I doubt if we can get a doctor's appointment on such short notice and on a Saturday, but maybe you could come to Elder Home and be examined by one of the doctors who visit. All you need for soccer, probably, is to get weighed, read the eye chart, and sit on a chair for an hour waiting to be seen. I think that kind of exam would do for your soccer team."

"I don't think an old people's doctor would be right for us. How could he know about our soccer muscles? He'd be looking for heart attacks and cancer, wouldn't he? An old people's doctor might even be a girl, and if it's a girl doctor, forget it, I don't want to be naked in front of her. And we need this done quick."

"Look, a doctor is a doctor. Drop the naked business. That's old." Richie has showed up in time to save the conversation. He brings news, he says, both good and bad. The good news is that Coach Dotson made appointments for them with his doctor, Dr. Towle. She's a woman. We may be able to check everything off the list if we keep the appointments.

"I don't mess with no woman," Andrew says in rap, but dead serious.

"Uh-huh, uh-huh, yes, you do, too/Or I'll bust your butt black and blue," Richie answers without pausing, then adds "If Coach Dotson can go to a woman doctor and take off his clothes, or some of them, I guess, depending on what's wrong, then you, you little nerd, can go, get a quick going-over for the soccer team, and you're out of there. Think about it and grow up. Try to. Well, Mom, that's the good news. We have appointments with this girl doctor, Dr. Towle, who Andrew is afraid of. I mean of whom Andrew, the Brain-Dead Boy, is afraid."

Richie has just studied "who" and "whom" and now is the grammar police, correcting "who's" and "whom's" whenever he hears them, whether they are wrong or not. He says, "wheum," and I don't think he always corrects us correctly. But it is nice to hear him use what he is learning in school.

"I am not afraid of any girl. You are," Andrew says automatically.

"What's the bad news?"

"My teacher, Ms. Vincent, who wrote you the note last week, wants a conference with you as soon as possible, ASAP. She says 'asap.' She uses initials for everything. Her dog is named Deeogee, which translates into DOG."

"Well, at least she has a dog." Andrew's words are ice cubes. He looks at me.

"Is this the conference about failing the drug test, and when are these appointments with the coach's doctor?"

Richie looks at his watch.

"The appointments were ten minutes ago, but if we hurry we won't be later than necessary."

Sometimes I think Richie states the obvious in ways that make it sound crazy. I hear myself working up to a yell about getting in the car and do we need any soccer forms for the doctor to sign.

It turns out that Dr. Grace Towle does not charge for lateness even on Saturdays, and she practices holistic medicine.

"Medicine with holes," Andrew says, as if he'd heard of it, and she laughs, encouraging him to think up other cute things to say. She wants to have a family counseling session before she goes ahead with the examinations. This is her usual procedure.

"The exams are only for the soccer teams," I say. "I know it's late, so maybe we can skip the counseling. Thank you for taking us as a favor to the coach."

"No problem. I have an appointment after you, so this time is free." She laughs. There's a glow, a ruddy one, about her, and she looks as if she ate plums and spinach leaves and nut bread. Because she is so friendly, her glowing doesn't make me envious. I bet she even jogs.

"So, you would rather not have a pre-examination counseling session? It's optional." She smiles. I smile back. We seem to be old friends.

"You are right," she says. "It would be silly to have a session when you are here only to get the papers signed for Coach Dotson. I get carried away. Please excuse me."

My heart is beating. This woman is the second honest doctor I have ever met. I have met some good doctors and some dedicated ones but, to this point, only one other honest one. Dr. Randolph told me to expect Mama to fall and break her hip, but he doesn't count because he went to divinity school before medical school and refused to overcharge, or charge at all many times. I know I have never met one who laughed at the profession. Of course, two things: it may be that I am thinking of the doctors who, or "wheum," I see at Elder Home. This Dr. Towle is not exactly a traditional doctor, she is, after all, a doctor with holes. Now, I'm thinking cute for her, like Andrew.

I continue checking out her hair and clothes. A bad habit, one I should be ashamed of, but I go on. I note her hair, which looks like pharaoh's sister's, black and shiny from that fruit-and-nut diet. Long fingers, even though they look a little chewed on. A gold chain bracelet and running shoes, plain cheap ones. I catch myself. I am a fool for impressions, first ones. I remember my dangerous tendency to idealize my opposite and I stop short.

"Tell me about yourselves while I look you over. Jump up here, Andrew."

Andrew leaps more gracefully than I've ever seen him, perches on her examining table, and makes a Mr. America muscle for her. "My, my. I'll have to come see you play soccer. When's your first match?"

At this point Andrew, who has never delivered a note or message, hands her a neatly folded schedule of games. One of his space figures, the ones he carries everywhere, falls out of his pocket. He picks it up and in the same motion, points to the first home game.

"You could come with Mom, there. She sometimes can come."

I begin thinking the way Dr. Towle is supposed to be thinking, but she is too busy being shanghaied by Mr. Cute. She's falling for him.

I go on professionally in her voice in my head: "This child is seeking a family unit, a vicarious family experience, in short, roots that spread out to the community. Your child wants his mother to have a friend, to drive to games with, to go out to a movie with, to call on the telephone, to enjoy little moments of life with, to have a context, as we professionals say."

Then I think like myself, mad at Andrew, "Whaddaya mean, *sometimes* can come to your games? I come when I *can* come, am able to get off from work early to come. Do you want to eat or have me at your games? Someone has to work."

All this is waging a small war inside my head. I need a Tylenol extra. I tune in to real life and hear the nice doctor saying, "You will be a wonderful sweeper or wing this season. You look great, Andrew

McFall. Maybe you could come over to visit with my son . . . would you like that?"

She hesitates and for a minute, I see a flaw in pharaoh's sister, this perfect girl-doctor. She actually looks vulnerable, slightly frazzled. I see that she is biting on the side of her thumb. It takes a child to make a dent in perfection. Maybe this son she is inviting Andrew to visit is not as perfect as his doctor-mom. Maybe this son has sent her out on a mission impossible: find me a friend. My movie imagination begins to unreel: this son is at home dying. Of AIDS, yes, or he has terminal leukemia and needs a friend to go down to the wire with him. His mother, poor thing, is desperate for a friend to take home to him to prove her love. If she can manage to take a name back home to him, a name like Andrew McFall, and even the promise of a visit, better, an overnighter, she will be in high clover, as Daddy used to say about things going well.

Dr. Towle twists her legs around each other and leans toward Andrew. I am not seeing things. She is a little desperate.

"Cool," is Andrew's answer. I could have told the doctor that and saved her some anxious seconds.

"He has a funny name." She still sounds a little quavery here because the subject is still her child, the one in the last stages of a rare blood disease.

"So do I."

"Andrew is not a funny name."

"To me it is."

She dies laughing. Why, is beyond my powers, but two happier people I have not seen for a long time. Andrew is, I can see, expanding his charm territory to the world of medicine. Teachers are not the only targets.

I interrupt at this point, or as Richie points out on the way home, I "mess up bad." It seems it's bad to prompt, to seem to rush into a friendship. Much better "to hang," to hang back.

"Ask Dr. Towle what her son's name is, Andrew."

"So, what's his name?"

"We call him The Wrench. Are you going to laugh at that too?"

Andrew looks as if he were conducting an orchestra. "No, I like it. I wish I had a nickname."

I can see another failing entered in the big book just outside heaven's gates—SHE DID NOT GIVE HER CHILD A NICKNAME.

Richie has a private session with the good doctor, so I have no idea what additional failings he points to in our lives. It lasts thirty minutes. Later I find out that a lot happened during that half hour. Our lives head in a new direction, you could say.

Andrew and I wait for him in the waiting room. Instead of reading the old *People* magazines, we stare at the state trooper across the little room from us. His brass nameplate says *Wilson T. Armentrout*. He is in full uniform, with two guns hanging in black leather holsters on his belt. But Andrew and I are embarrassed to stare at the person sitting next to him. Glances tell us that he is a convict. He has real handcuffs on and a little chain between his ankles. He's the one we want to stare at.

The only good thing about the situation is that I feel exactly at one with Andrew, an eight-year-old who is just understanding, beginning to, that there are things in the grown-up world that a person cannot look at directly. It's an instinct that develops late, like a twelve-year-old molar.

Officer Armentrout sees us staring at him and not staring at his companion. He laughs. We hear the leather creaking as he adjusts himself in the little scooped-out orange plastic chair.

"This is my prisoner. Broke his finger this morning. Hold up your broken finger, Alonzo."

Alonzo holds up both hands, with a smile as broad and friendly as Officer Armentrout's.

"My pinkie," Alonzo explains.

"How did you hurt it?" Andrew whispers.

"Don't ask, son," they say almost in unison, as if they had been asked before, an inside joke. Then the officer goes on alone: "The doctor works on prisoners. She'll fix him up, won't she, Alonzo."

"She has before." Alonzo grins. He has an Old English *A* cut in the side of his hair. The prison must have a barber who knows the latest styles.

Out in the parking lot, we see the state prison van with a wire mesh barrier between the front and back seats. It looks like a cage. Andrew explains to Richie that the convict Alonzo has to ride in the cage.

On the drive home, Richie says that in his session with Dr. Towle she invited them to come home with The Wrench after the game she promised Andrew she would come to. Here I mess up bad again.

"Did she ask me to come too?"

"No, Mom, poor Mom. No, Mom, you don't get to have an overnight with The Wrench. You have to find a grown-up person to be friends with. Dr. Towle doesn't count because she will be fixing pizza for us kids. She's a mom-type. You aren't. You have your moments, though, good moments." He grins. "You could take the opportunity to have a d.a.t.e., as Ms. Vincent would say. You are getting so forgetful, Mom, poor Mom. Remember, we want you to meet the drug expert? Also, have you forgotten that you are *supposed* to go have a conference with Ms. Vincent ASAP?"

"What would you do without the word 'supposed'?"

"Make up one, I guess. Why do you want to know?"

"I just wondered."

"You think a lot, don't you? I like that, Mom. Really, I'm not kidding. Oh, I asked Dr. Towle if The Wrench wanted to come over to spend the night with us. Okay? And then she invited us to go bike riding with The Wrench. She said he would provide the bikes. They are big into bikes and all that stuff and I thought it would be nice for us to develop new interests."

"You haven't even met this Wrench. How do we know he's not a murderer or has something wrong with him, wants you to steal for thrills? Aren't you rushing into things, not hanging? Biking is not just riding on the sidewalks anymore. It's with helmets and astronaut energy candy bars."

"Get real, I mean, grow up, Mom. You are going off again. You're mixing The Wrench up with the prisoner you just saw. Alonzo Johnson. I got his whole name from Dr. Towle. You are too impressionable, too afraid of things. You worry too much. This Wrench guy's a kid. He's ten, between me and Andrew. His mom is a doctor. You met her. Does she look like the mom of a murderer or a thrill seeker or klepto? You've got to chill out a little. Don't assume the worst about people. You may be a little jealous of this kid, this Wrench guy. And biking is just like soccer, I mean it's got a modern version of itself, that's all."

He has me on all counts. I assume the worst about too many things. But to hit on a kid I haven't even met is a new low. Grace Towle, "call me Grace," looks more or less perfect and has a healthy attitude toward people, even prisoners, children, and work. If I don't watch out, I will begin not to like her before I even know her. I stop myself with a jerk: *here*—I put my index finger on my left temple—is my tendency to suspect anyone who seems well adjusted. Grace Towle can treat the broken pinkie and not get mixed up in whether it got broken in an attempted murder. The broken bone with a Latin name would be her problem, not crime in America. She certainly wouldn't be prejudiced against a child because of his weird name; in fact, her own child has one of the worst names I ever heard, though in my family there are some real wingdings. Cecil Dunn Pelot, I guess is the worst one, and poor Cecil has lived down to his name.

So I say, "Go bike riding with The Wrench and ask him to come over to visit. It will be nice to make a new friend. I'll call his mother and invite him over." This attempt at being broadminded brings screams and groans. Richie and Andrew know I do not sound like myself. A little too relaxed, too hanging loose.

"Mom, Mom, Mom, look in the mirror. It's the police van. The officer is driving and the prisoner is in the front seat with him, not in the cage. Slow down. The red light is flashing. I think he wants you to stop."

I look in the rearview mirror. Andrew is right. Richie is saying "Cool, Mom. What were you doing wrong?"

Nothing. I wasn't doing anything. Not speeding, not swerving, not wrecking. I pull over to the side of the street. I watch Officer Armentrout walk toward us in the side mirror, and I can see the prisoner grinning too in the slanted mirror. He waves the splinted finger as if he were a famous person waving to strangers. I don't wave back. Richie and Andrew crane around and wave furiously to Alonzo, then turn toward Officer Armentrout.

"Don't worry, Ms. McFall. I just wanted to tell you that your license sticker has expired. I didn't want any of my buddies to stop you. Actually, it was your friend Alonzo Johnson—we call him Dr. Johnson because he goes to the doctor so much—there who noticed it. You ought to see about it. That's all. Have a good evening, now."

Then he turns away from me. "Boys, Alonzo says hi to you. He also wondered if you wanted to write to him in the city jail. Some schools do that sort of thing. Tours, too. If your teacher wants to bring your classes on tours, Dr. Johnson conducts them. You'd have to see one to believe it. When his hand gets well, he wants to write to outsiders. If I can ever be of any help, just give me a call. Armentrout, Officer 711. Easy to remember, almost 911."

Richie and Andrew nod their heads like crazy. "We want to," they say together. I say thank you and drive away three hundred years older.

On Monday, a week later, in the conference with Ms. Vincent, an older black woman, I learn that Richie is an overachiever who is trying too hard. If only he can learn how to relax, how to enjoy being a child, Ms. Vincent will feel better about him. He always volunteers to do all the extra work, write all the skits and plays for the special programs, clean up the art room. Anything that calls for responsibility, Richie is there. He has started a Write-to-a-Prisoner project that all the students are really into, and as wonderful as it is, it may be too much. It's good to worry about people like prisoners and victims in war-torn countries, but really, don't I think, these are concerns for us, the adults.

"Does he talk about a prisoner named Alonzo Johnson? And is it a real problem, this taking on responsibility, for Richie in school? Isn't he on the honor roll?"

"Yes, he is. But as you know, children try to fix the world for their parents so the parents can be happy. Their efforts take a great toll on them, and the parents, not you, my dear, but most parents, I am afraid, never even notice the weight the children carry. It's invisible to them. I'm not saying it's invisible to you, my dear. But I have wondered if this prison project weren't an expression of your son's anxiety? I do not want to alarm you, but I wanted to talk to you. Offer some TLC. Excuse me for talking in initials. I sometimes forget how to talk to adults. And yes, Mr. Alonzo Johnson is the incarcerated resident's name with whom we have been corresponding."

Ms. Vincent leans across her desk and pats my arm.

It is news to me that Richie is carrying the world on his shoulders— it seems he also organized relief funds for Ethiopian children—but Ms. Vincent's sympathy for Richie is so strong, so intelligent, like Dr. Towle's, that I begin to have a bad feeling toward her, even when she admits to having some flaws. Am I jealous of my own child, my own poor little baby, for his getting to be the center of attention?

I get ready to leave, and Ms. Vincent smiles at me and says, "I know it's hard." That's all she says, but I almost hug her for it. There is only one thing more she could say that would make me "fine," as Andrew says.

She could tell me that researchers have proved that migrant children, gypsies, in-transit families, nomads, American bedouins, do better on standardized tests, in fact, on all tests, than stay-at-homes, one-placers, rooteds. But you can't have everything in one conference. Richie has an expression to describe the best girls, the best women, he knows. He hasn't used it for me, just for teachers and girls in his classes. "She is a goddess of queenness," he will say. When I was with Ms. Vincent, I felt I had reached the lady-in-waiting level.

A picture of Richie going to his first day-care center pops into my head and almost knocks me over. His little shoulders slumped, he tottered into the center, which sounded like an ax-and-anvil factory, so much noise was coming out the yellow door. At that center, the director started teaching the alphabet to eighteen-month-olds. Those who weren't interested in ABCs were in trouble and were recommended for testing. It was a nightmare for me. Andrew's day cares were too, but I had learned by then to find a babysitter, a grannie type who would take him into her home and let him live a little life with her all day—soap operas, washing dishes standing on a stool, talking on the phone to her friends. In some ways, I could see, with Ms. Vincent's help, that Richie had had a tough time. I remember once a long time ago he patted me as Ms. Vincent had, right at the elbow crook. "Don't worry about me," he said in baby talk. I guess I believed him.

"Any advice?" I ask, but do not mean it sarcastically. I hope Ms. Vincent will have some. She does. At least she tells me her secret for relieving children of their worries, the invisible ones, for a few minutes, which according to her is a long time in child-time and the most we can expect. She plays music for Richie's class, real music. Last week she chose Handel's "Water Music" because it is so "sprightly"—her word. The children renewed their energies and strength listening to it and she did too. She will lend me a tape, because, of course, we adults have invisible burdens too. She laughs a big warm laugh that gets me to laughing too.

Then she brings up an incident, the other side of Richie's burden-and-responsibility-seeking: Richie brought in a gizmo that, he explained to the class, was what real criminals use to break the locks on bikes or car doors. Like a letter opener, she says. His report was supposed to be on the rising crime rate in America, but Richie seemed to know a little too much about the specifics of crime, the MO. Do I know about anything that might shed light on this? Here, for the first time, Ms. Vincent does not sound sympathetic. Richie's report turned into a demonstration of how to crack a lock. The students loved every word and crowded around him. Richie can make his reports so real. You are there, he begins, she says. With the bike he brought in, an expensive one, she is sure, he demonstrated how the lock could be broken, quickly and quietly. She is willing to let him do this demonstration for a special assembly perhaps, but she does not think the classroom is the place for teaching criminal techniques.

"Did you know he had this lock-breaking device?"

"No." I don't even know where he got a bike to use in his report. I say no, I didn't know, again.

"Parents know very little about children." Here she laughs again and so do I. "Teachers may know even less."

I am in shock. First, I meet a doctor who asks questions, invites my children to meet her son; then I encounter a friendly, civic-minded convict and a helpful officer of the law. Now a teacher who doesn't know everything. Am I on earth?

"I'm glad Richie has you for a teacher." I am about to cry.

"Oh, I am glad he has you." I want to hug Ms. Vincent but think the classroom is not the place for hugs. She shakes my hand and pats me again. "Come back," she calls as I leave.

~~~~

In a week, The Wrench calls us to invite the boys (but not me) over and to repeat his mother's invitation to go bike riding. When I answer the phone, a voice with a funny accent, not any I know, asks to speak to Andrew. "This is Wrenn Chauncey Towle," the voice says. Then, "The Wrench is calling Andrew."

I do not meet The Wrench face to face under the best circumstances. On their first outing on rented touring bikes, which Richie and Andrew have never ridden, they have a serious accident. That's what Officer Armentrout calls it. As he is driving down old Route 1, he sees a tangle of bikes by the road. He stops, recognizes Dr. Towle's boy and his friends, and calls me at Elder Home. I get there before the ambulance. My scraped, bleeding, white-faced boys ride in the ambulance too, can't walk, they are so shook up. I am furious when I see the bikes. These are the real things, with upside-down handlebars, little attached leather bags behind the seat, thin tires, and water bottles with siphons on the frames. They are long-distance, serious machines, suitable maybe for the Tour de France. One looks like the bike Ms. Vincent described, the bike Richie used in his report on crime.

Andrew and Richie have never ridden anything (that I know of) except old, broken-down three-speeds. It is a miracle they aren't all dead. I am happy the bikes look ruined. Their price tags skitter through my head. My first impressions of The Wrench seem correct: he is dangerous, maybe not a murderer, but a killer biker.

Dr. Towle comes to the hospital. Her face does not glow and she looks ready for institutionalization, as Ozone Layer says. There is a mixture of fear and anger written all over that pale face. There is a coffee stain on her white jacket. She hardly notices me, not that I care, before disappearing into the emergency room. It's one thing to have a kid in the hospital when you are a doctor; it's a whole new ball game when you are an activities director for old people. It's one thing . . . I realize I am working myself toward migraine city and I cannot afford to do that.

In a few minutes, Dr. Towle is back. Her first words are "The Wrench fractured his collarbone, one of the most painful of all breaks."

I stare at her hard. Surely she will not make me *ask* about my children. She will know to tell me about them. She cannot be that dumb about a mother's needing, craving, to know hard facts about her children. I am glad her son is alive, sorry he has a broken bone, but let's hear a word about my kids. Internal injuries. Were there things I couldn't see with my untrained eyes as we rode to the emergency room?

Simultaneously, as if reading my mind, Dr. Towle says, "Andrew and Richie are banged up, but not broken anywhere. They can go home with you." Then she loses that professional look and speaks more or less in my language, the one I call Hopeless.

"I am so upset with The Wrench. I know he wrecked—almost on purpose." She looks haggard.

I know it too but don't say so. I'll repay the favor of seeing her surface crack a little and be kind.

"You know The Wrench has a lot to fight." She looks at me for agreement, and I, who have only talked to this child on the telephone and ridden with him in the ambulance, for some reason do not say anything ugly back the way I want to. Mama always pointed to Thumper in *Bambi* as the best of examples for human relations—inadequate most of the time, I have found, to the situations in my life, but one I sometimes fall back on: if you cannot say something nice about someone, don't say anything. I nod a slight nod, my head beginning to thump harder.

"He's not a biological. I mean he is adopted. And I am single. Not divorced, single. I have chosen parenting but not marriage. All of these circumstances are hard on The Wrench."

I know then that I am not dealing with a whole deck. The Wrench and Dr. Towle deserve each other. I don't have time to think about this pair. I have a pair of biologicals. Children of divorce, to be precise. They are mine, blood and bone. I am not a doctor with great earning power and with immediate and natural access to emergency rooms. I ask if I can go back to see my sons.

"Of course," the doctor with holes in her head says.

IV

$\mathcal{T}$he Wrench's stay in the hospital lasts three days; then he goes home. The boys call him and our telephone rings a lot. They take him some of their homemade cookies—they select and buy, then slice and bake, the frozen rolls of dough. He has the most formal telephone manners I have ever heard, and I have talked to more officials than I like to think about. "Mrs. McFall, this is Wrenn Chauncey Towle," he says each time. "May I please speak to Richie or to Andrew if it is convenient?" I am used to hearing my boys eat on the phone while they answer my questions in grunts and mutters. "Are you eating celery?" "No, just chips."

I know we have reached a new level of friendship when I answer the phone one night and hear, "The Wrench here. Richie home?"

The Wrench becomes a big part of our lives, at least a big part of the boys' lives. I guess they introduce him to their father while I'm at work. He seems to know everything about us and uses extreme tact avoiding certain subjects, like dogs and fathers. He does not have either, it turns out. He wants a dog, but because his mother is away so much, they have decided to wait until their lives are more "composed."

The Wrench talks like a forty-year-old, but he can talk in other ways, too—I hear wild laughter from the three of them when they don't know I'm around. He spends nights with us, a first in all our moves. His mother is on call at the hospital several nights a week.

"You can laugh around me," I say.

"Oh, yes, we understand that." The Wrench is polite, as his aide-de-camp Andrew nods. Face it, I am a damp blanket, but they tolerate me, and Richie and Andrew do stop eating when they talk on the phone.

The Wrench is a very good name for a person who is, in many ways, a monkey wrench, though I must admit, not all the time. I am getting over the bike accident as his collarbone heals. He is small for his age, but he has a large spirit. Andrew, two years younger, is much bigger.

Grace Towle, with all her medical training, must not know how much junk food is necessary for American children. In fact, she nearly won me over all at once when she praised me for having such large, such tall, children.

I take full credit for their genetic endowment. I mention to her one time what we have for a typical supper—a large can of ravioli over corn chips with nacho sauce to top it off. There is a long silence. So, having an advantage, I go on about Richie's fried-egg-and-baloney sandwiches, his grilled peanut-butter-and-cheddars. Another long silence, but it's over the phone so not too awkward.

Dr. Towle and I are becoming friends, I guess. Grace and Ruth to each other. There is a Grand Canyon between us as people, but her tiny adopted black-eyed son, who holds his wrists up and shakes them as if he were beginning some ancient ritual and has the most eloquent of shrugs, has brought us together and we try to make the best of it and to see the pros in each other. I need to know her better before I can ask her why in the world she got into this single parenting of her own free will. I am into motherhood thanks to biological fate, and my imagination stops cold at the thought that someone would choose the life—even with only one kid and thousands of advantages, like money and a medical degree, for starters. We live across a canyon all right. I am mad as fire at the world on my side, and over on her side she is having a good time in the world. I am not surprised to find out that she watches birds for a hobby, but I am bowled over when she invites me to go on a walk with her local bird-watching group. I want to say into the phone in a chilly voice that I do not have time to watch birds. They can watch me if they want, feel free. But I don't say a word when I see Thumper looking at me and saying hush. I accept the invitation but dread going. Trees and birds are in my past. I don't want to get too close to them.

Driving out of the city, I let her go on and on about the way birding helps her. I keep the ugly thought to myself that she needs a little help, but when I see birds fly through the woods toward the caller, flutter toward us as if we were nice big friendly nuthatches or hermit thrushes, I feel help flying in toward me, not just to her. The sunshine and the sky tilting behind the birds through the binoculars Grace hands me lift me out of my life of problems. It really seems as if the woods are moving toward us, and I stand there waiting for them.

Andrew and Richie keep bringing up the subject of my meeting the drug expert, Douglas P. Smathers. I feel that we have enough new people in our lives, with Grace and The Wrench taking up more and more room. The boys explain that he will not be a new person after I meet him, just as Dr. Towle and The Wrench are no longer new. Would I set a date, please? The please is The Wrench's influence.

Me on a date? I never had dates. Just times to meet Rich in the woods. The first time we dressed up to go anywhere, just us two, in public, was the day we got married.

Where we did go, separately and from different directions, from ninth grade on, was to the 1941 Buick, a Torpedo model, blue, abandoned in the woods near the Tar River. An old junked blue car lowered into a grove of poplar and beech trees—no way could it have been driven into those woods, the trees were too close and too big.

An alien dropped it down in 1952 when it was already old, did some sci-fi magic—sucked in the steel sides and squeezed it between the trees. We made up this story. The car had just shown up, cartoonlike, to make us happy. The whole world, in fact, had sucked and squeezed itself into secret, accommodating shapes for us.

"We have a car, all right, but we don't want to go anywhere," Rich said. We died laughing at our good luck. Our car had already been everywhere, to Mars and back to us.

Ninth grade. In September, one Friday night, sex took over where our galactic games left off. The car became our motel room.

If Richie follows in our footsteps, he has only two more years of childhood left.

In the car's "yard" I skinned the squirrels Rich shot, chopped up the onions and potatoes I had taken from Mama's kitchen, and fixed us a feast. We wouldn't eat with anything but what we found—old broken parts of plates, two bent spoons. Fried squirrel won Rich's heart the way that mule on the fire escape had won mine, chained me to Rich, not forever, as I used to think, but for a long time.

I was never afraid of blood or guts, a characteristic that caught Rich's attention. I was the girl kneeling over a dead squirrel with a hunting knife, the girl turning a squirrel wrong side out, and I guess I surprised him. Phyllis was his ideal. Mine, too.

"You can't be in my homeroom, or Rich's, if you don't pass," Phyllis said to me, her voice like new grass in a breeze. She knew this was a death threat for me.

I told Phyllis everything—except about the Buick, the squirrels, and, of course, later, the sex.

She told me everything about herself, except the same big fact I didn't tell her. Her plans to be an interpreter for the UN, her aunt paying her way to Tulane, the vinegar wash for her hair—that's what made it burn your eyes in certain sunlight. I should try it on my brown hair.

I loved to spend the night with Phyllis. Her house, the old Joyner house, was built in 1797. "There were still Indians around then, just a few, but yes, around here, and that year Wordsworth was writing *Lyrical Ballads*," she would say, amazed that her house was part of what she loved to study, brushing her black hair with the red sunspots in it even at night. She wore cotton batiste nightgowns with eyelet sleeves. I wore Daddy's old T-shirts.

The house was brick, six bricks thick, with deep-set windows and a balcony that no one used because it might collapse.

We both took for granted in our long nights of talking that she and Rich would get married. She laid out her plans for her life while she brushed her hair, then added, "You should plan your life," gentle as ribbon. "Don't jump into things."

"I don't know how to plan it," I would say.

"First, you have to go to college. I will go to Tulane, Rich will go play basketball at Chapel Hill, and you, Ruth Elizabeth, must go somewhere."

"I promise," I said in my semi-innocent way.

"Look at the girl," Rich yelled, meaning me, from high up in our sycamore tree, our lookout tree. He scrambled down the tree, almost without touching it, ran over to me, grabbed my hands, slick with squirrel blood. "I'm going to marry you. You can skin squirrels for us forever."

He looked crazy and my heart was beating against my eyes. That was the first time, the Friday in early October, four years before I was pregnant with Richie. A miracle not to be pregnant every one of those months.

Whenever I skinned a squirrel or cleaned a fish with Daddy's pocket knife, Rich would do a crazy boogie on the roof of the Buick and scream up at the trees that he was going to marry me.

"Sure you are. I believe that."

I never said I was going to marry him. I knew he had to marry Phyllis. I wanted him to. Sex was something that belonged to us in the woods, at our hideout. It was not ours in the real world. I didn't want it, not Rich either, in real life. I wanted Rich and Phyllis to go on with their lives, their plans for the UN and the orchard/law practice—they had so many plans, detailed ones. I thought Rich and I would get over the sex, like the measles, and we all could go on with our lives, the right ones. I would think of something for me to do. Friendship was as important as love to me. I loved Phyllis as much as Rich. I bet it's true for more people than just me. And as the criminals say on my TV shows, I didn't mean for things to get screwed up, to get out of hand, to go wrong, for any of us to get hurt.

I try not to think of cleaning fish when I fix frozen fish sticks for the boys. I don't want them to know all of my talents. They would love to learn to fish and hunt, but not in this life, not with me. It's all I can do to be Ruth Activities at Elder Home. Fishing and hunting are activities from my past. I'm reincarnated now, a new person. Almost a new person.

I wonder if all this sounds crazy, what my new friend Grace Towle would think, this story of how Rich ended up with the wrong girl. This story of how I ended up becoming a migrant worker, so to speak, with two children, all because of a mule on a fire escape, a skinned squirrel, and an old Buick.

Richie says "sick" when he means "crazy." I agree—it was all a sickness, a disease, and I think the three of us had different strains of the virus, the secrets we kept from each other, loving each other, everything.

"You have to marry Phyllis, who is perfect." This was my answer to Rich as he danced on the roof of our car. And he would answer, even before he finished dancing, "I know it."

After that first skinned squirrel, I didn't have to keep on almost killing myself trying to impress him. I didn't have to run across train tracks just in front of the train or lie down longways and let the train run over me. I just skinned squirrels or cleaned fish. Once he shot a deer and I helped him hang it up and dress it.

"You sure are a different kind of girl. Not like my old lady, the librarian."

Rich's mother smelled like coffee and old books, sharp and dusty. She wouldn't charge fines if she thought you were really reading your overdue book. People lied to her all the time. She was the type who couldn't bring herself to cut up a chicken for supper, much less a squirrel, with the fur, sometimes mangy, and intestines still inside him. She wrote poetry and loved Phyllis. They read *The Atlantic* together. She was a strange one for North Carolina. Mama would shake her head over Mrs. McFall.

Rich hunted, I cooked. Rich and Phyllis led their lives of dates and school, and Rich and I led our lives in the woods.

With me, Rich had a home in the old car, one that didn't cost anything; it was nice and quiet. We never talked, we were so busy with our little adventures. We built a raft. We never thought about current events, or anything real. There could have been a nuclear war for all we knew. We didn't listen to the news from Vietnam. What did we care? Phyllis knew all about the war. She seemed to absorb all the bad news, so we didn't have to think about it.

No movies or proms for me. Rich took Phyllis on dates. They looked official together, stamped in heaven. She starred in all the plays, won all the beauty pageants, went to all the honor club stuff. She was in the newspaper every week for something she had done. She was straight-A smart, read everything in the library. She was the sweetheart of the prom our senior year. I waited up for them to call me, to hear how dumb it had been. They were my public life. I was their private life, at least I thought I was. I never thought, never dreamed, that they had a secret life.

Too stupid to live, Daddy used to say. We didn't know who he meant. But I apply that description to me during those years.

I want Richie and Andrew to lead public lives as teenagers. Go on dates and to every prom within driving distance. Like Rich and Phyllis, but without a lost person in an abandoned car, a squirrel skinner waiting for them. Soccer, school programs, anything out in the open.

~~~

It's ten-thirty when I leave Elder Home after my slide show, "Wildflowers of Virginia." It's the treat I'd planned for the residents after we got through the inspection. We are working our way around the United States in Activities—wildflowers, rivers, birds. I promise to tell them about my bird-watching experience, about the red-shouldered hawk, the way the expert could whistle and make sounds like rustling leaves, the way the sky seemed available for a *drink* of pure blue. They like for me to talk that way.

When I get home to the door I hear snarling and laughing, a weird combination. "There's a dog in there, there's a dog in there," I yell through the door as I drop the keys, hating myself for leaving the boys without a babysitter. Aren't they old enough to stay by themselves for two hours? Sure, their father might sneak in and cook them something. So what?

It sounds like a murder going on full speed. I pick up the keys and open the door, saying over my shoulder to nobody, "Puppies, that's no dog. You've got puppies in there."

Right. There are two puppies, big black ones, tearing around, trying to strangle each other with their open jaws. Richie and Andrew are lying on the floor, laughing in long barking yips.

The puppies, big teenager puppies, not little cute ones, stop jaw-strangling each other, look at the laughing boys, and jump, all four feet in the air at once, on top of the boys and try to get their jaws open wide enough to get their full set of teeth on the boys' necks.

I start screaming. Puppies, not dogs. Where did they come from?

Dumb question. They are going to the pound in the morning or right now, late as it is. We can throw them over the fence there; they are not staying one more minute.

"Look, Mom." Richie stands up and straightens his sweat pants. There's a gash on his cheek and his new soccer shirt is ripped. He is beautiful and happy, as happy as the Virginia children in the slides holding up armloads of wildflowers and singing, it seemed, "The Hills Are Alive" with Julie Andrews.

"Dad brought them for us. They are like, just like, the ones he had when he was a kid. Dad had black Labs just like these. He thought you might let us keep them to grow up with."

I splutter and can hardly get my breath. It's a lie. Rich never had a dog, much less puppies. His librarian mother was allergic to dogs.

That was one of the "terrible" things about his childhood, he always said. No dogs. He used to go on and on about it. He wanted hunting dogs. I had dogs coming and going, and I can't see that I'm a better person for the experience. And Rich's childhood was so much better than his own children's, but does he know that? Imagine having a librarian for a mother and a man who owned orchards and who wanted you to study law and run an orchard for a father.

Andrew says we should shut the puppies up in the kitchen for the night with newspapers on the floor, a bowl of water, and some food. Rich had brought a bag of puppy chow. Thoughtful of him.

The boys get the dogs calmed down and locked up in the kitchen.

I get my breath back. If I tell the boys Rich lied about these puppies' being like his boyhood dogs, I will be the bad guy, which is my usual role, and after I tell them their father never had a dog of any kind, they will still want these puppies and throw fits when I drag them off to the pound in the morning. I can't win.

How can we have puppies in an apartment?

"It won't be too bad, Mom. We'll do all the work. We'll take care of them so you won't even know they are here. They'll teach us responsibility." Richie is working himself up to a full-scale fit. Andrew chimes in, "Yeah, Mom, yeah, responsibility."

I go to bed in my own bed without speaking to the boys. They try to look upset but are so glad to have the puppies even for one night that they let smiles quiver on their faces, the way water brims in a glass when they fill it up and walk across the room with it saying, "Not a drop, not a drop."

In late October, we still have the puppies. Richie named them Elder and Home. They sleep with me sometimes. It's like sleeping with two baby seals. I can't get up at night and roam around the apartment or crawl in bed with one of the boys because I will wake up the puppies and then it would be play time and we'd all be up for two or three hours.

The apartment smells like Happy Jack dip. I have a patch of mange on my elbow that the vet laughed at, saying he kept a patch himself, that I should just call it the heartbreak of psoriasis and let it go. Dr. Towle says it will dry up in a while. Before Christmas. The Wrench approves of the dogs.

Richie is set to do his drug-pusher act as part of the Parents Be Pushers Back, or PBPB, program. Ms. Vincent says Richie can get the kids' attention, but more, he can make the parents really listen to the facts about the dangers of "our drug culture." She goes on too long, like a teacher. Drugs are "worldwide," she says. "Drugs and education go hand in hand, in a way." She thinks Richie's natural gift for acting should be put to good use. In fact, sometimes she thinks his abilities to act go unappreciated. I can tell she thinks a great deal of Richie goes unappreciated.

No one mentions the drug expert who dresses like an undercover agent anymore. I think the dogs have taken the boys' minds off getting Mom a date.

Richie knows that Ms. Vincent asked me about putting his act into the Halloween program for his school, and he has polished it into something that could be a television commercial. Andrew is proud of his brother's talent and wants to get there early to get a good seat. "It's not Broadway," I say.

"Mo-om," he yells in two syllables, washing oceans of shame over me. "Richie needs us to back him up."

More and more, Andrew smells like the puppies; dog fragrance hangs in a brown cloud around him. When I sniff him, loud and obvious, half kidding, he just says, "Responsibility. I smell like responsibility."

"Responsibility" is a word that always sets me off.

Maybe dogs are the answer.

I am getting a headache, standing at the sink with my hands balled up into fists jammed into the dishwater. I can hear myself in my head, my voice getting louder and louder the way it always does when I get close to the night I finally left Rich, threw his grandmother's ring out the door into the mud, bent Andrew over my arm like a load of dry cleaning, and left the old trailer near the tobacco warehouse.

The past is dangerous, a poisonous fog, like in an old horror movie, rolling in from a deadly sea, and sometimes I cannot stop its coming in and covering me, swallowing me and all my little efforts to make a new life.

One night Grace calls and says she has her iced mineral water by the phone. I say I have my glass of wine. She asks if I will please tell her about Andrew and Richie's father. She has heard fantastic tales from The Wrench. "Would I mind?"

I launch into my story, keeping my eye on the clock on the stove. It's eight-thirty. "I probably wouldn't have left Rich, wouldn't have known how to walk away from Rich and my secret sweetheart past, my whole life, if he hadn't been drunker than usual, whispering all kinds of things—about the old Buick, the fried squirrel, the good times we used to have. It'll take a long time to explain all of those things."

"Where were you living then, Ruth?"

"We were in a trailer park outside Durham. Rich was hunched over the tiny dinette set. I had opened the bills—rent, heat, and electricity—and put them out on the table. He muttered he'd quit his job—this one he'd lasted in three weeks, the one at the lumber yard that made me hope I could pay the biggest bills."

"How did you pay them?" I can tell that Grace is interested in my story in a different way from all the counselors I've talked to. She wants the facts, but she is sympathetic. I can't help myself and start throwing in some special effects.

"I yelled out the amount on each bill, but he kept on whispering to himself something about how I was the lucky one. Phyllis, he groaned, was the unlucky girl. 'How's that? How's Phyllis the un-lucky one around here?' I was really mad then. All Rich could do was repeat how unlucky Phyllis was."

"Did you have trouble carrying the babies? I mean with your pregnancies, Ruth. Were you able to eat properly?"

"I worked until the day before each boy was born, if that's what you mean. No, I felt fine as far as all the physical stuff went. But it got so I hated to go home, to pick Richie up from the babysitter. I never knew what I would find when I got there. I couldn't take it anymore. Rich would get drunk and yell that love was dead and that didn't help much either."

We both laugh at this and I am surprised to hear something amusing in my story. I think about repeating myself, just to hear Dr. Grace Towle laugh—it's a warbling blend of colors very like one of the bird songs I want to memorize.

In a lighter voice, I get to the worst part of my story. "I told Rich, 'Go get Phyllis, then, go get her back now. Love is dead here, you are right. Go get your official girlfriend. It's only been six years that you've been married. Go back home and find your real sweetheart. Make her lucky, go marry her.' I kept hoping to jerk his attention to the bills, even after it sank into my brain that he'd quit this good job of running a forklift to carry the logs at the paper mill."

"I think you are remarkable," Grace says, this time serious as night.

"Then I started stuffing baby things and my clothes into a garbage bag, Richie's clothes and shoes. I guess I had tried packing up too often. If we had to live under a bridge or in the woods, I was leaving this time, I yelled."

"Did you mean it, Ruth? Would you have lived under a bridge with two children?"

"I think I meant it. I really do."

"You are a brave person."

Grace Towle's admiration is making me drunk. I have hardly touched my wine. I wheel on, a bird flying toward the expert caller.

"So I stuffed the clothes into bags. I was determined to walk, then run away. To walk across the cracking ice of the past that Rich was groaning about, his head down on the table, his words slurred into one long groaning whisper about us, the three of us, Phyllis, Rich, and Ruth. I was yelling that there were two more of us now, forget high school counting, and we needed a roof over our heads and some food from the grocery store, real food, not squirrels full of shot. Frozen pizza or fish sticks would be nice, some canned spaghetti."

The doctor murmurs something about how glad she is I was concerned about nutrition in the middle of this terrible crisis.

I ignore her emphasis on health care and get to one of the worst moments. "Then Rich kept whispering at me, 'Two babies.' I said to him with the bags by the door, 'Yes, you've got two babies if you can call boys six and two years old babies.' I remember saying this, picking up speed as I ran over the ice of our past, which was making terrible noises cracking."

"Did you actually think your marriage would last forever? You know that two out of every three fail. That is one, I emphasize *one*, of the reasons I have chosen not to marry. But that is another story. Please go on, but wait, please, until I get a refill of water."

As I wait for my friend to get her glass of imported water, I answer her question for myself with that nice live-phone sense of knowing someone is coming back to hear my story.

Until that night in the trailer in Durham, I had thought, too-stupid-to-live me, that Rich and I had a past, a secret life, that would hold us together through anything, our fights, his quitting jobs. Our secret sweetheart sex in the woods had magic powers. The old car, the squirrel blood, all that. I thought the explosion into "public life" when we got married, even though I was the wrong bride, that the event would somehow weld us together. The heat of the shock to everyone, including us, would turn us into some kind of metal couple on top of a wedding cake. It was crazy. Sick, as Andrew says.

All the plans he and Phyllis had to marry after college were the same ones I had for them, until I got pregnant. Then I changed. I wanted to get married, period. Being pregnant was real life. Forget Phyllis, who had just been his paper-doll girlfriend, no sex, just dates. She would understand, would have to, that a baby born to an eighteen-year-old girl in North Carolina needed to be born to married parents. Simple thinking. Rich had let me know in a thousand ways that Phyllis was a virgin, it was part of their master plan for their lives. So Phyllis, I thought, could go on with her plans for Tulane and the UN. She could marry a diplomat, one who read *The Atlantic,* who loved poetry.

"So what happened then?" Grace is back on the line.

"I'll have to tell you in the next installment. I think I should save the worst part to tell. It has taken me a long time to really understand what had happened to us. I thought for a while it really was unpaid bills and babies. I knew Phyllis had what we call at home a break-down, but I didn't understand the whole story and I guess I can't tell it all in one piece, so it makes sense anyway."

"Well, we have a long time for stories, not tonight, Ruth, but in our lives, I mean. What did you do right then? That night?"

"I ripped my wedding ring off and yelled something about being sorry he had not married his Phyllis. I was sorry, very sorry. I wanted to walk away from that trailer, out into the rain, and die under a bridge somewhere. Get lost."

"Did you leave that night?"

"Oh, I left and have been leaving, trying to, since. I don't know if you can understand about childhood sweethearts, especially secret ones. Romeos and Juliets, only we were living in North Carolina. But I can't get drunk and cry, as Rich did that night. I am not free to live in a van like some hippie who doesn't know his time has passed."

"No, and you were not free to study medicine and then adopt a baby as I was. Andrew and Richie have to grow up. They need a few years of 'time out'—that's what one of my textbooks called it—from their parents' past. They don't have anything to do with, really, the Buick car, or Phyllis."

We are on the same wavelength. I swallow a small amount of my wine and say, "I see my duty as a mother to take them away from all that as fast as I can."

"You are doing a good job." We say good-bye. I am happy and can hardly understand it, but I feel the way I did when the birds were flying toward the caller and me from high in the branches. The trees rustle. I feel the sun. I do not have to go on with the long story that replays in my head whenever it gets a chance. I feel free not to think of when Rich and I got married—the one time we had gone out on a date. I thought Rich chose me—maybe because of squirrel blood— to marry, not Phyllis, the perfect girl, the virgin. Anyway, I was pregnant. Phyllis could go on with her life, somehow, I felt. How was I to know she was pregnant too? I didn't know about her baby until sometime after that night in the trailer, when the rain fell in sheets on the metal roof, six years after our wedding. Putting it all together took a long time. "Babies, babies," Rich kept saying, crying and whispering. He didn't mean just the two boy babies we had. He meant the one Phyllis was pregnant with when I was pregnant with Richie.

I will have to explain all this to Grace, how we were a trio, Phyllis, Rich, and Ruth, a threesome in a terrible, grown-up way. Only then I did not know how terrible. Phyllis thought I was simply Rich's friend out in the woods building things, her friend to talk to. I thought she was his bride-to-be, when all their plans were ready. It was Rich, only Rich, who knew all the facts.

Grace will listen to this story and I will feel like an expert, a wonderful feeling, even if I am an expert only about my own life and its troubles.

I will tell her more than just about that night in the trailer, the bills spread out on the table, that minute before I left with Richie and Andrew. Maybe to Grace it will not sound "retarded," as Andrew says about anything strange, not to have known, not to have suspected, the truth, that Rich and Phyllis were leading their own private one-of-a-kind life too.

I think she will like to hear about our place in the woods, the fried squirrels, the faded blue metal hood of the Buick, the lookout sycamore with the platform built high in it. All those collapsed into each other the night I left. The nights I spent with Phyllis, the long talks while she brushed her hair, were not true, were, in fact, nights when she and I were both busy distracting each other from the truth. I was not the person I thought I was then, not Ruth the wild girl, not Ruth Elizabeth, best friend to Phyllis, not Rich's true sweetheart. Rich was not my true sweetheart, Phyllis was not my best friend.

When I tell her, Grace will be able to ask the right questions about the baby Rich kept whispering about, his head down on his crossed arms on the table. I bet she will point out how that baby is or was Richie and Andrew's dead half brother or sister. I can tell her sometime, I think, about how Rich lifted his head and yelled in a high cracked voice, "Two babies then. Another one later makes three." I didn't "hear" it for a long time, but it registered somewhere deep inside me. She will be struck, I am sure, about how at that moment, even though I didn't know what he meant, just that he was dead drunk, I opened the light aluminum door to the trailer and threw the ring that should have been Phyllis's as far as I could.

And she will be struck by the perforated ulcer the emergency-room intern said I had. She will understand why I signed Richie and Andrew over to emergency foster care for two weeks. Rich never forgave me for doing that, having the ulcer or signing those papers. She will ask me questions I have never found answers for about Phyllis and Rich, who did not have an old car in the woods.

Maybe the doctor and her textbook training can explain to me about how Rich could think he could have Ruth or Phyllis, river sex or jungle sex, river bride or jungle bride. I have always suspected he thought I might kill myself if he left me instead of Phyllis to get an abortion or have a baby by myself. Pregnant me kept him out of the real rivers and jungle of the Mekong Delta. But pregnant Phyllis would have kept him home too. I don't know why he decided to marry me, have our baby. Maybe it didn't matter, maybe he thought I was the cause of all the ruined plans and he might as well try this kind of life.

Dr. Towle may point out that Rich, at least as she understands him through my stories, would have almost enjoyed the war, wouldn't he? Trekking through the jungles, eating fried tropical squirrel, rafting down hot brown rivers? I will say, "Yes, I think he would have been right at home in a way over in Nam."

Dr. Towle will have a name for what I call Phyllis's going crazy, having a breakdown. I will say, "But she didn't jump out of a tree, kill herself," as I would have done if Rich had married her and not me. At the time, right after we got married, when I heard Phyllis had been committed to long-term care in the state hospital, I thought it was her genes, and it's true they played a role, because her mother went crazier and crazier in the old Joyner house, wouldn't come out of the basement, wouldn't eat, probably got worse when she understood what was wrong with Phyllis, why she wasn't going to Tulane to study languages. I didn't know about her abortion. I thought it was her broken heart, that I had broken it by marrying her Rich. It boils down, I will say to Grace, one expert talking to another, that Rich married me, lucky river-me.

Many times, though, I will admit to Grace, maybe when we are ninety and roommates in Elder Home, I have occasionally envied Phyllis for the secret abortion I finally came to know must have taken place, the state institution, the years of . . . what? I did not know and don't know now and can hardly imagine. But I got married, okay, had two babies, okay.

Lewisburg, Roxbury, Sparta, Norway and Denmark, Highpoint, Durham—I've tried the small towns and now I'm trying Richmond. I used to choose places in North Carolina for their faraway-sounding names, hoping for some kind of escape from Rich and the past.

"Don't worry, be happy," I murmur to my greasy dishwater.

I try to do something practical at moments like this when the past begins breaking up in big icy chunks and, more dangerously, melting into a poisonous fog, moving in on me.

Make some curtains for the window, the dog window, I call it, in Andrew and Richie's room. This is a project that will keep the fog out. The ceilings are high, the window must be fifteen feet tall. I've never seen such a tall window, with three long sheets of glass, a solid upper sash and a split double pane for the lower, no curtains. It would take ten yards of material, and to special-order it, the woman at Sears said, would cost $115.00 and take three months.

Dog curtains. Make curtains. Somehow, curtains will help things.

Still, normal life, great as it is with the puppies and our new friends, is not all that great. That's Richie's expression, "great, not all that great."

On the outside, children look beautiful, have ocean eyes like Andrew or Indian-length arms and legs, like Richie, but they are really—pardon my French—not always so great. I get the feeling that the doctor, even with a near-perfect child and career, may understand this expression.

And mothers sometimes don't look too bad either, especially in this time of all-age dressing in Reeboks and jeans, and with permed hair. But secretly the mother, no matter how slim and jeaned, jobbed and benefited, is struggling to control the arrhythmias in her chest and stomach. In good times, her heart beats slowly, not scraping the ribs or falling down on her stomach, like right now, when they are going into a spin cycle together.

The boys are sleeping all night like normal kids, without their mom sneaking into their beds to steal some of their whatever it is kids have when they are asleep. That halo of smell around their dirty hair? I am more normal, sleeping with the two dogs, talking on the telephone as I drink one glass of wine.

They are sleeping, I am sleeping. The Wrench stays over when he feels like it and his asthma is not too bad. The puppies are making a nice adjustment to sleeping first with the boys, then with me. We are in separate beds and rooms. The curtains are hanging unhemmed, waiting patiently to be hemmed by me crawling along with my needle and thread or lying on my back sewing upside down. Next, I think I'll try wallpapering as a move toward homesteading. Stability.

Elder and Home watch television with us. We are normal, I think, for the first time in our lives. Monotony is an unclaimed prize in life, believe me. A boring routine holds the heart and stomach of a mother in place.

Soon, Andrew and Richie will learn to hate our normal life, and they will call up good old Dad and have him bring in their orders of pizza or corn dogs, ribs and subs, the minute I fall asleep or go to a slide show or night activity at Elder Home.

But for right now, it's great that they are not staying up all night to raise the window so Rich and his dog can come in to eat or play with them. So far as I know, anyway. Great that they aren't arranging for me to be gotten out of the way, taken on a date with an under-cover type. Great that they have made a friend.

"Brush your teeth," I say mildly to Andrew.

"Why, where are we going?"

"You don't brush your teeth just when you are going out. Brush them for staying at home. We have to look at you." Andrew looks at me as if I were speaking Japanese, but he listens, and later I hear some lazy swishes. Then he brushes Elder's teeth, but says Richie must take care of his dog's teeth. He can't be expected to brush his and Elder's teeth plus Home's teeth, it wouldn't be right.

"It's not right to brush any dog's teeth."

"Why not?"

"They don't eat candy and drink colas, so they don't need to clean their teeth."

"Elder loves Snickers and Cokes. She ate three yesterday."

Normal life explodes into the old life I'm used to—me yelling about wasting money on dogs, money I do not have. If we ate chicken every night, we'd have better teeth. The last dentist trip cost $67.00, just for two cleanings by the hygienist. The puppies need spaying—which will cost $83.60 each and will be coming up soon, when they are approximately six months, or we'll have puppies having puppies—plus shots, shampoos. I have spent $237.21 so far on the dogs, and we are not even close to the operations.

"I don't want Elder to have an operation. She would love to have some puppies, and I would help her take care of them."

I jerk Andrew up and, eye to eye, yell into his face, "NO, NO, NO."

"Okay, okay, take it easy. Mom, you should try to be a little chilled out. All I was doing was telling you how I feel about my dog; she's not beautiful, she's just a little pretty. You like her and you know you'd love her puppies."

They are sleeping so hard—I guess from all the fighting and extra soccer practices and taking the puppies out to play in the park—that I have been able to think about having, for the first time, a new kind of life as a single parent. Night life, even dating is a possibility. I am getting closer to calling the drug expert man.

Maybe somewhere there is a grown-up who would like to have a date with me, my sons and dogs. I will not fry squirrel or go to an abandoned car or try to kill myself to attract a little attention. I will act my age, thirty, which I cannot believe I have made it to, put mousse on my new frizzy hair, iron my jeans, and maybe invite this Douglas Somebody to give a slide show on stars or drugs on a specific night, which I will put on my Activities bulletin board for Mrs. Osborne to check out. I will have to learn to say "shit" in the modern way, the way I hear all the young women say it, punctuating any story, any remark, with it. "No shit, good shit, pile of, you're shitting me"—the meaning is carried in the tone, in the content of the story. I never have learned to talk that way, to smile sweetly or questioningly and say softly, "Shit."

I am thinking crazy. Dr. Grace Towle doesn't say "shit" and I have not heard any of the birders say that word. Back to curtains. Hem them without taking them down. Kneel on the floor, contort myself backward with a needle and thread and hem away. Now and then, I catch glimpses of myself reflected in the window. Not bad, except I look glassy-eyed.

I know what that glassy look—the dead look—is from Elder Home. Mrs. Osborne saves money by not calling the doctor when someone dies. She just calls the undertaker, who has something worked out with the doctor. What's the point of calling the doctor, she wants to know. And it gives me another "activity." She thinks there's no point to having activities for people who aren't "really people" anymore, so if she can find something practical for Ruth Activities to do instead of spelling bees and Bible quizzes, trips to greenhouses and museums, poetry contests, journal writing, then she can tolerate my presence— my bulletin boards of birthdays of famous people and our residents, the craft fairs, the rhythm bands. So I am the one who straightens the dead people out, changes their diapers, fixes the beds, closes their eyes, wipes them off, so they'll look better when Mr. Pearce comes to undertake. I decide that I should ask my new friend Grace about whether I am breaking any laws about dead people. Do I need a license or something official to close their eyes?

It frightens me to see Richie do things that are like Big Rich, even little things. Like talk on the phone. Rich would brace himself against the wall with one arm, hang his head down, and cross his legs while he talked on the telephone. He looked like a man being tortured. Richie looks the same way.

Once Rich tore a phone out the wall when it rang late at night. The minute it rang he would start cursing as if someone were kicking him, then give it to me to answer and stare at me as if I were a snake while I tried to talk. He said it was the worst modern invention and we should fly black flags on Alexander Graham Bell's birthday. He said hell was full of telephones.

But I must be careful not to see talking on the phone as a sign of more than it is. I think Richie knows there is one way, a better way, to do things. He would think one way home was better, not the same as any other way. He would stand on the muddy riverbank, ask Evaldo if he knew how to walk through the jungle, and then plunge into the vines, not the river, and get home. He would not think either way was okay, like Rich. There is just one better, safer way home. Richie would take it if it killed him.

By Halloween night, the curtains in the boys' room are hemmed. I feel safe. I feel in control of things. Almost in control—I have a date.

This undercover expert in drugs, Douglas P. Smathers, will meet me after the Halloween program on drugs at the school. We will set a date for his Elder Home talk.

Old as I am, I don't know how to act on a date. Find a tree to shinny up and jump out of onto the branches like a flying fool? My Elder Home residents can be my role models. I'll act the way they do at the socials I rig up for us: I'll dress carefully, put a sprig of something on my collar, put on a little too much of my new lipstick—Mango-Mango, it's called—then rub on some cologne from the sealed package that came to Resident, 2-A. I won't go so far as to wear health sandals and stockings with toes. I will have to go on a health program before I can even think of using Grace as a model for how I want to look. Drink that fizzed water, cut down on the coffee and wine and candy bars with Elder.

No one tells me everyone is dressing up in Halloween costumes for the parent-teacher meeting, so I am the only one who looks weird. Andrew always looks as if he were in a costume with his stone-washed jeans, his surfer T-shirts that hang out below his holey sweat-shirt, and his Mohawk haircut, the one I sent him to get, thinking at the worst he'd come home a punker, with just some green gel in his hair. Richie is backstage. I am sitting out front waiting for the big moment when the curtains open.

"Why doesn't anybody tell me anything?" I am talking to myself. The answer is obvious but hard to say back to myself.

I'm feeling pretty good despite my Elder Home style and give myself a B minus for momhood. I am supposed to meet My Date after the program and go out for a beer while the boys help Ms. Vincent clean up.

On the radio coming to school, I heard the star man, the man who runs the Star Gazers meetings. "Antares is in Scorpius in the early night sky. Look carefully," he says, like a teacher. "It's sandwiched between Saturn and the moon."

"That's interesting," I say to the radio, practicing some date-talk for later.

Andrew is patrolling the auditorium, inspecting the costumes. He fits right in. The crowd of ghouls and ghosts are holding hands, proud parents. I sit tight and watch Andrew. Behind me there is a big maple tree. Some nut has tied branches to himself, lashed big limbs to his chest and back and down his leg. He doesn't have a face, just leaves glued on around his eyes and then flowing into a long red beard. He's a swaying orange-and-red tree, really beautiful, though the leaves are touching my hair and I feel as if I'm in the shade.

When I change my seat, the tree, a little later, moves with me. I get up and move to the back of the auditorium. The tree follows. This happens twice. The witches and clowns, hoboes and cats, let me by them when I move. The kids are GI Joes, Jasons from the horror movie, Draculas, and Frankensteins.

When Andrew swings by, I hiss at him. Why didn't he tell me about wearing costumes?

He doesn't know exactly. The Wrench's mom doesn't have a costume on either, he points out. But it looks as if she does, I say, with her white jacket and blood pressure gauge hanging out of her pocket. He shrugs. I wonder why The Wrench isn't there, or is he, in disguise. Andrew says he's been sick with asthma again and sent his mom to see the program for him. Then Andrew sits down by the tree, who stretches his branches around him.

I'm not going to move again. I say this to myself, then I repeat it out loud. It sounds like something from the Bible or outer space, very important, deep, dark words.

Andrew leans forward. "Say what, Mom, what did you just say?"

"I said I was not moving again. You stay put, and tell your tree friend to stay with you. I don't like being followed."

"You got it, Mom." When I turn around, I see Andrew looking happy, his face half hidden in the leaves of the tree.

A man dressed in red maple branches for Halloween? Not a bad idea. Break off a few limbs, tie them on, paste some leaves on your face. Cheap, inventive, natural materials. I could have gone as Dog-Woman, if I had known it was a costume party. All those dog-hair balls under Andrew's and Richie's beds to stick in my big hair. My black leotard and a tail pinned on. I could have been Lab-Puppy-Woman. And Dr. Towle, her costume was a natural too and gave her a great advantage in talking to the teachers, not that The Wrench ever needed a parent-teacher get-together about his work or behavior. I can see her talking to people dressed in recycled things.

Richie is onstage calling the audience to order. He is at ease and acts as if standing in front of an audience of over a hundred people were part of his everyday schedule. When we are quiet, he begins:

"All you parents, from all around,
Listen up, listen down.
Check this message out:
Kids don't want them things around . . .
You the ones, uh-huh, uh-huh,
Can run this town.
Mom and Dad, or just one,
Take some time. Have some fun.
Go to games, go to school,
Go out camping, know this rule:
Kids don't want them drugs around
You the ones, uh-huh, uh-huh,
Can run this town."

Richie is on between acts—students reading their essays on drugs or showing stagewide murals that they slowly unroll. One class does a puppet act about kids capturing a drug pusher, only the puppets are kids with strings working their arms and legs. Then Richie comes out dressed like a drug pusher, a rapper, all glitzy and "bad looking," he says, in one of his raps, and does another verse. The audience loves him. He is the star. The tree-costumed person stamps his feet in time to Richie's rapping.

I must be the only person on earth who hates trees, especially maples, not the cute sugar maples with buckets and red plaid people stirring pots nearby, but the North Carolina variety, the Florida maple. I am the only person, I am sure, who has fallen out of a tree—it was a Florida maple—during the act of love. That's what Rich called sex when we were in high school. When we were married, he didn't call it anything.

I fell out of trees other times, many other times, when we were building our platform, which was intended to be a skywalk in the trees around our hideout.

"Slow down, girl. You're not going to last very long if you keep breaking yourself up by falling." Rich laid a carpet of moss under the walk, tried to get it growing, and some of it did, but most of it turned into dry powder, though one patch of British soldiers, the moss with the red heads, survived the transplant, I think because I watered it.

The worst fall was the act-of-love fall. There's a third board to turn back onto, I was thinking as my right shoulder went down into emptiness.

Crashing down through the yellow and red leaves, too shocked to scream, I missed the moss, both the soft green cushion and the dry ashcake stubble. I was sure I had broken my knees, but I knew I wasn't going to the hospital naked. Getting my jeans on was harder than having a baby, which is a slow wet pain, not the dry cracked bone feeling.

Comparing pains is one benefit, I guess, of getting old. At Elder Home the residents love to play one-up in suffering:

"Papa died of peritonitis."

"It was the flu of 1917, I was seven and waiting on everybody in the whole house."

"I lost three of my babies."

"The bone was sticking out, white as the sink."

"Mama swelled up like she had swallowed a pumpkin. She burst open in the night."

They can go on for hours. I should make it an Activity and give a prize to the survivor of the worst pain.

"Get up and walk," Rich said, as if he were Oral Roberts or Jesus.

"I can't get up. My legs are broken and I don't have any clothes on."

"Hold still. I'm going to slide your jeans up your legs and test the bones as I go." Rich was careful as a doctor. After any trouble he caused or helped cause, he was sweetness itself. In fact, his mother called him Sweetness, and when the basketball team heard her slip one time after a game, "Sweetness, we'll see you at home," they picked it up. "Slam it, Sweetness. Sink it, Sweetness." Rich didn't mind—Rich or Sweetness, either name got his attention.

Maybe a shrink would say I almost killed myself on purpose around Rich, falling or jumping when there was nothing to fall from, just to bring out that sweetness. Maybe I got pregnant to keep his attention for a little while. Phyllis did not have to get Rich's attention. She had it and she had mine too. She was like a lighted window to us, calling us in from the woods, saying it was time to come into the house and sit down for supper and talk in long, calm sentences. "Despite" was one of the ways Phyllis began sentences.

Now, years later, the poem we had to memorize in third grade seems sinister: "A tree whose leafy . . . a tree who in summer wears/A nest of robins in her hair/A tree who looks at God all day . . . Something, something, a fool like me." Joyce Kilmer got the fool part of the poem right and I am sure it's maple trees in the poem. We had nests of whippoorwills, not robins, near our skywalk. They flitted around like big brown moths.

Rich lived in trees fifty percent of his life before we got married. Now the van has replaced trees.

"I am a tree man," he'd say and mean it. "That's why I'm a great basketball player. I owe it all to trees. I think tall, am tall, play tall."

Three generations, going on four, he said, had owned orchards, McFall's Apple Orchards, that ran in wide contours over the county. Rich slept in the apple trees except in the worst weather, and sometimes then, wrapped up in black plastic.

"It's one of my talents," he said. I've seen him sleeping, one arm hooked over a branch, lying on his side, a foot jammed just right into a V of limbs, his other arm folded into a pillow.

We could make love in a tree because to Rich a tree was a bed. I went along with the idea even though we had just started building the skywalk and there were only two boards nailed down in the first tree, the maple he called Big Red.

"You're lucky you didn't get a nail in your skull," he said as he was lifting me up and working me down into my jeans. He sounded as if he didn't have anything to do with my falling. He had grabbed a limb when I dropped out of his arms down through the leaves; then he snaked down the tree feet first, taking steps as if there were steps in the air to come down alongside the trunk. I can't imagine Rich falling out of a tree.

I hit our pile of slabs. It wasn't quite dark. We had been working on the board walk up in the branches for two hours. I was perspiring but the pain froze the sweat dry.

I did get up and walk. After forty-five minutes. Rich felt every one of my bones, slowly and sweetly. When he finished, he said, "Get up and walk," and I did, slowly, like a very old person.

"Damndest thing you ever saw," his father would say and bring in people to see his son sleeping in a tree. Because Rich didn't wake up until he was slept out, many people had a chance to see him, dead asleep, along a limb, like a caterpillar. They would stand around under him, talking in normal voices about the frosts, the rains, the packing houses. Rich did not wake up. Trees, he said, were his friends, better than people. Never talked back, swayed in the wind, had babies every year, looked good, never asked for anything but earth, air, and water.

"Do you like trees better than me?" I asked him one time when he was on a roll about them.

"In some ways" was his answer. But he grinned and grabbed my knees, tackled me down like a kid brother. "You are going to kill that girl," his father would say when Rich would tackle me out in the orchard as a change from running the spraying tanks.

"No, we're just playing," I would say, even though one time my shoulder was dislocated.

Trees were his brothers and sisters. His pets, his dogs. His mother, the librarian, thought books were the only friends anyone needed, but she didn't mind trees, which were no threat to books. She thought it was good that Rich had two human friends who were girls and such different kinds of girls, too. By friends, I think she meant no sex. And she meant girls who wanted everything for Rich, no matter what.

Rich read in trees, kept his books stuck in them. The orchard was his library. "Tolstoy over there, Dostoyevsky over there"—he'd point—"in alphabetical order, backward, in plastic baggies."

Their only child, he was going to inherit the orchards, and they raised him like a tree. Their secret message about the world must have been something like this: There's nothing to life but standing and waving yourself around, displaying yourself. "How tall and beautiful!" I think that's essentially all they ever said to him, or "Damndest thing you ever saw." Maybe "Have a drink."

Around our abandoned Buick, the walk ran high in the trees, like a ramshackle castle battlement or a drunken catwalk. The blue Buick was almost dead center in the lopsided circle of the walk.

The woods were full of junk like old refrigerators and furniture, dragged off from houses on the highway. Rich had plans for us to scour the woods for living-room furniture. We did find a sofa in pretty good condition, but it had snakes in it and I said no.

"You can't complain about snakes living in that sofa. They found it. It's theirs. Finders keepers."

"I just did complain," I said and won the argument, shocked to disagree with Rich. That was the only time I remember fighting him until after we were married. We never used the snake sofa for anything but looks. And Phyllis, the only person I wanted to see what we had done with the encampment, never came.

"Knock it in tighter, but keep it straight." Rich had a level, with a bubble in a tube, to tell him whether the board was straight before he nailed it.

The boards slanted up to connect to the next limb, stretched down to a branch, only two planks wide in places, five in others where we could lie down, high in the night woods.

We memorized the order of the trees we chose for the skywalk: Big Red, the maple, first, then the sycamore because it was the easiest tree to start hoisting the boards up into. Up a little incline, we walked with our arms held out, like tightrope walkers, to the beech, dangerous because the brown leaves, which had been a dull blue-green, were so thick they got in our eyes. Then there were three poplar trees that Rich had to build a cantilevered wedge onto because the branches started so high. Four more sycamores that Rich called Brown Balls because they shed so many. Two old live oaks, weeping away, ended the walk. The white hickory trees were in a grove a little way off.

"Tie the rope tighter on the slabs," Rich yelled down to me. One slipped loose and grazed my head as I guided the bottom end while Rich pulled them up. It took three months of working after school, plus weekends, to build the walk. I had sap in my hair for weeks, until Rich stuffed it up in a baseball hat.

A slab would fall and almost hit me or glance away. "Serves you right for tying the rope sloppy. Could have killed you," he'd say into my sticky hair, taking the baseball cap off.

"Let's bring Phyllis out to see our skywalk. She'd be impressed." I was whispering into Rich's ear.

"No, let's wait until it's all finished, the whole camp. She would think we were crazy at this point. Anyway, she hates ticks, remember. Her uncle or somebody died of Rocky Mountain spotted fever. Apple trees in an orchard are about all she can take of the woods."

"I didn't know any of that."

"I guess not," Rich said, turning back to our work.

An old sawmill had a pile of slabs, bark on one side, rough cut on the other, so we had as much lumber as we needed. Rich wanted to build a cabin, then a village with a few high perches in the trees for lookouts. We started with the twelve trees in the circle around the old car, set like a piece of blue gravel in the ring of trees. Our skywalk was just the beginning.

It took twelve pounds of ten-penny nails to build it. My hands were torn up and hard as canvas from working on it. We never did finish it.

Time was harder to get than nails or tools. We bought time with lies. Mama thought I belonged to every club at school and played sports. She no longer went out of the house by then, so she trusted me to come home when I could. I would cook ahead, so she could warm up little pans of chipped beef or meat loaf. If she hadn't been sick, beginning to move slower and slower with inflammatory arthritis, I could not have stayed away from home so long. Illness took away her fight. She was much easier to live with sick than just worried sick.

Not that I was living at home. I was living with Rich in the woods. Making love on a skywalk, in the chilly dusks of that last fall of high school, I would try to see the stars, but the leaves were so thick they darkened the sky. When the moon was full, there was a brightness to the dark space beyond the leaves.

"I want stars," I said once.

"Why on earth? You got me, babe."

In the woods on the skywalk with Rich, I got the false impression that sex was natural. Not in the sense that the Family Life classes said sex was natural, and not the way the biology book explained it, with all the diagrams of reproductive systems. I wish I had paid more attention to the "Fertile Periods" section, which I can see now. I thought then that sex was natural, meaning fate had you by the throat.

"Fate is sex or fate is sexy," Rich said one night and I can't forget it.

Pine splinters in my back, poison oak up my neck, broken blisters on my hands, sprained wrists from holding the boards while Rich found the best place to nail them to—all this hard work and pain made me think what we were doing was what we had to do. I didn't learn until I had two babies how social, how *chosen* instead of natural, sex is. How connected it is with money, housing, jobs, education, and natural disasters.

"Damndest thing, I could hear the gypsies feeding, could see the leaves disappear." This was the last thing Rich heard his father say before he drank the chemicals that would not kill the moths.

I can't explain what happened to us that year, even though I lived it, our senior year. The gypsy moths came—the earliest invasion by gypsies into North Carolina, and the first recorded attack on apple trees—Rich's father killed himself, Phyllis and I got pregnant, Mama got slower, and Rich and I got married.

The night before Mr. McFall drank the insecticide, Rich and I were in our usual place up in the trees. Now I know it was my "fertile period." Richie was conceived that night, high in the darkness, in our last happy time. Sometime that month, that terrible month, April, Phyllis conceived her baby, the aborted one. Where, I don't know. On a date, I suppose.

"Stars don't give a damn what we do. I wish people would learn this." Rich spread his grandmother's quilt, the wedding ring pattern, doubled and folded again, on the wide part of the walk. We were looking up at the stars blinking through the ruffling sycamore leaves, some as big as dinner plates. Rich could run the skywalk, grab the limbs.

Rich laughed, hard, then left me to climb high in the nearby white hickory tree, yelling Tarzan yells. This was the last good time. After the orchard was ruined, Rich didn't have a plan for his life. No trees, irrigation, orchard management. He didn't think anyone could teach him anything he didn't know already about trees, especially orchards, but he didn't have anything else to do after the orchards were ruined. No orchards, no plan.

He follows us in his van, on automatic pilot—I'm his past, I guess, what's left of it.

The audience wants Richie to do another rap or repeat all his in-between ones as an encore. He agrees to do some parts, but it is clear to me that he has prepared an encore that recaps all his major points about parents and pushing.

"Push your kids on the street.
Don't you worry about *whom* they meet.
If you love them, if you care,
They'll come home, stay in your hair.
Remember now, I told you true—
Drugs are a substitute for you.
Push kids out to make new friends,
Send them out, do not cringe.
Let them go. Don't say no.
When you push, you pull them in.
When you push, you pull them in."

This brings the audience to its feet. Parents are smiling and getting their coats and bobbing and murmuring about pushing kids out and pulling them in. Richie has cheered up a cafetoriumful of people.

"You're Richie and Andrew's mother. I'll wait by the trophy case," a voice says over my head. It's a voice without an accent. I stand up and walk away from Andrew and the tree, saying over my shoulder to Andrew that I will see him and Richie in thirty minutes.

I had told Douglas Smathers on the phone we could have a thirty-minute date after the program. His answer had made sense to me: "Thirty minutes is half an hour." I said, "Right." We seemed to understand each other. He looks the way his voice sounded on the phone. Most people don't look like their voices.

I want to say to the audience as I'm leaving that I am Richie's mom. I am kin to a star. I say to myself that I've figured out that Rich is the Maple Tree Man. Instead, I say to Andrew, "Tell Richie to ask Ms. Vincent to come to supper next Tuesday. I'll fix pizza."

My "date" gets to the trophy case first through the crowd. He is an undercover type, looking like one of the real parents but without the costume. He smiles at me. I am sorry Ozone Layer can't see me, but I'm glad that Andrew and his tree friend can. I wonder if my new friend Grace can see me, but because she looks right—in costume— because she probably brought some nuts and dried apricots for refreshments, and because she obviously got a note from school carried home by The Wrench, I do not want to see her. I avoid her. I am beginning to feel that I have told her too much about my life. It's embarrassing that she knows about my last night with Rich, about my past. She's got to return the favor, cough up her story, so we'll be even, not that her story could be much in terms of being embarrassing, in my book.

When I walk past Andrew, he leans away as if I needed more room. I think I hear Andrew saying to the tree that something about me looks different.

*F*rost lies under the trees in the school yard, so it looks as if a pale icy curtain had been flung over the branches, its edges dragging on the ground.

As always, I stare at the other parents, so nicely married, not like me. And not like Dr. Grace Towle, but she evidently chose not to marry, chose The Wrench from a line of orphan-filled baby cribs, chose to be a doctor, chose to live here, chose everything, as if freedom were the air she breathed, unlike the air I breathe.

Holding hands as they leave, thinking about how much potential their children have, how nice to have them on the honor roll, in the talented-and-gifted program, invited to enter the computer fair, the parents hurry home to read bedtime stories to their kids. I try to pretend I am a nice parent, one of this crowd, hurrying to a nice home.

I hope Andrew's teacher has seen me at the program. She was backstage, I guess. She must have been, but I am not sure because of the costumes. To hear her talk, as I did in our last conference, her whole life is her students, like Ms. Vincent's. Andrew is her special concern.

"He is a heartbreaker." Ms. Sowers had looked at me to see why I had made Andrew into a heartbreaker. I didn't exactly go for that description of Andrew, but it's hard to interrupt a teacher on the subject of the need for individual attention.

"Andrew makes desperate attempts to catch my eye, no matter how, no matter when. Once he cut himself on a rope by winding it tighter and tighter around his wrists. His hands were blue when I came running out on the playground to see why the children were screaming for me. I wouldn't be surprised if Andrew doesn't have a more severe learning deficit than the one we are already aware of. He must be overcompensating for something. Don't you agree?"

I just sat, glowering, like the troll monster-mom Ms. Sowers saw in me. She went on.

"I know he wants braces on his teeth."

Here I had to break her flow and say that it was news to me and I bet to the dentist. "Andrew has teeth like marble, and coming in straight."

"I didn't hear you," Ms. Sowers said.

"I guess not," I said, plain as Dan Rather.

That conference was not a success. I came away sick with myself and hating Ms. Sowers. I have called her Lemon Sours in my mind since then.

Nicknaming is a habit left over from Rich. He sometimes called me Rue, as in "With rue my heart is laden . . ."

Maybe Ms. Sowers had dressed up like a lemon or grapefruit, but then I think I would have known her.

I try to think about how beautiful the frost is, like a lace edging to a tablecloth or a big curtain, ruffling alongside sidewalks, gravel, the asphalt, near the trees. The star man on the radio ended his program with a note about star frost, as if he had actually been to a distant star and returned to do a show on the subject.

"In the early morning, the frost follows the shadows thrown by the trees and in the bright sun, the frozen shadows are incredible to see. Yes, there is frost on the stars."

"Okay, I get it. Frost is special," I say down in my turtleneck and through my hair. I can see now why frizzy permed hair is popular with us thirty-year-olds who have a lot to hide, to filter, to screen. Hair is a natural hiding place.

"Yes, it is," my date says.

It isn't as bad as I thought, meeting a date. Of course, it is only going to be a short date to talk about a slide show for old people.

Why did I promise Andrew he could stay behind after the Halloween program and clean up the stage with Richie? If he wants to clean up so bad, he could have walked home with me. There is plenty to clean in the apartment. The bathroom looks like a wrecked boat, everything wet and washed to one side.

Does Andrew think he has to do exactly what Richie does? Richie has been coaching him on acting drunk. When I throw a medium fit—they both look so much like Rich, soft-shoe staggering—they think I am being mean.

"It's role playing, Mom. It's to help kids understand alcohol abuse. If they see us reeling and rocking around, under the influence, they won't want a drink or a hit of something. Would you rather I teach him to rap or break locks?"

"Grow up." I sound foolish.

"Don't go off track, now, Mom." They practice where I can't see them now. I ask them if they could help me do CPR demonstrations in resuscitation—I had to be certified in it for Elder Home. "You can pretend to be dying."

Andrew calls it artificial suffocation, and when I laugh and say I hope not, he never smiles.

They could clean up all night at school for Ms. Sowers and Ms. Vincent for all I care. I am so mad at both of them they could spend the night at school. They never mentioned that grown-ups would be coming in costume. They never clean up after the puppies, Elder with her mange and Home with the heart worms. I know Rich is not going to pay the vet bills. I was the only mom at the program in plain clothes, and I was the only one who didn't bring refreshments.

Instead of planning a slide show at Elder Home with my date, I begin telling him my troubles, the immediate ones.

"One mom, the ballerina, said we were supposed to bring nutritional things this year. She carefully unpacked her veggies and yogurt dip. 'Didn't you get the letter last week explaining the dress-up PTO meeting and the kinds of snacks we could bring?' 'No, I never got a letter.' 'Oh, you got one,' she said sweet as pie. 'Your kid just didn't give it to you, but you got one.'"

I go on to my date about how I wanted to rip her tutu, and then she added that I had two boys, she believed I did, so she was pretty sure that I got two letters. She had helped stuff the envelopes even though she was running a temperature of 101 degrees. I don't know why my friend Grace hadn't told me about the letter, the costume, the health-nut refreshments. I go on for a while.

Douglas Smathers looks pretty caught up in all this, so I go on some more with what I said and what she said. 'Yes, I know it is Halloween. Yes, I know that, but this is a PTO meeting, and about serious stuff—drugs, crime, heavy stuff.' Ms. Perfect Mom just kept on ar-ranging the broccoli and carrots in the shape of a witch's hat."

Douglas laughs a nice laugh and says he loves walking when I suggest one of my good ideas—walking home, leaving the car at school, and then walking back to get the boys and the car. That will be a two-mile walk. Exercise. It is trendy, good parents do it, every-one on TV does it and in the magazines. Even at Elder Home, I give my oldie-goldies exercises—neck moves, finger bending. Gerry-danc-ing, I call it.

The night is getting quieter and quieter as we get farther away from school. The chill reminds me of another October night. Douglas Smathers doesn't seem to mind silence and scuffing leaves, walking in the dark. He seems to have his own thoughts.

I had spent that terrible October night alone in our little asbestos-shingled house, pregnant with Richie, sure that my new husband was dead in a ditch, his dangerous spirit rising up, an amazed ghost, from a four-car pile-up. Some stranger's children flung all over the high-way. I was cold, but I wouldn't turn on our space heater. I was trying to save electricity.

It took me weeks to calm down, and Rich held it against me that I couldn't eat or sleep.

Where had Rich been? Just taking a friend, Brian Humes, whose engine block on his rebuilt '54 Fairlane had cracked, to Meredith College to see his girl. Brian didn't have the lucky break of being married to his sweetheart. I should understand that. I should really understand that violent need to see someone. "It's called love, Rue," Rich said.

I didn't yet know, of course, that Phyllis, my co-sweetheart, or co-dependent, as one counselor called her, had already had her abortion and was drugged and tied to the bed in the state hospital at Windsor while I was acting out a real life sit-com about young married life: pregnant bride, drunk, bored husband.

I think some of those trips Rich said he made for Brian were in fact trips to Windsor to see Phyllis in the hospital, tied up and drugged. These are things I have figured must have happened from the hints I got from Mama about Phyllis.

I am beginning to hope that he did go to see Phyllis. But at the time, I could not stand it that Rich would leave me a prisoner in that little house for whole weekends. I was too proud to beg him to stay home, me the tree girl, the wild girl. But I wanted to scream for help.

"Help" is not a word adults use. Kids use it in games all the time. Help, the ship is going down, the Indians are coming closer, the transformers are losing power. But only in accidents, when windshields are shattering, do grown-ups use the word. But "help" is often the right word. Help, I'm tired of eating instant oatmeal for three days. Help, I have headaches all night. Help, the toilet's leaking all over the trailer. Help, the phone's been disconnected. Help, Duke Power cut us off.

And if help had come to the little house? Nothing could have helped me, because what I needed was a whole new life. A new childhood leading up to a life different from the one I was trapped in. I did not need a bag of groceries, or a phone, or a plumber, or a doctor—not really.

Thinking about Rich was dangerous. Living with him had been worse. It had driven me crazy to have real danger brought into our lives, once Rich and I were married—danger for its own sake, not just play-danger, not just falling out of trees or cutting a hand while skinning a squirrel. But it was danger that Rich felt was the essential ingredient to what he called our little two-by-four life. Sometimes when I would threaten to leave, he would fall down crying, grab my knees and say he was going to kill himself. On that October night in the little asbestos-shingled house, I was not ready for his act. Later, in the trailer in Durham with the two boys and him talking about babies, I was ready to leave. I had printed the suicide crisis number on the back of the electric bill with red Magic Marker and stuffed it in his hand. I should have left that October night from the little house before Richie was born.

"We should be living close to the bone. I want the boys to live authentic lives, Rue." Rich would repeat this, scratching his arms, which were covered with red-blond hair, with his open pocketknife. "We aren't leading real lives," he would say, staring at the fake pine paneling, the wall he put his fist through twice.

I think his ideas about danger were set in concrete, confirmed, when he read Hemingway in the one night course he took.

"Go catch a big fish when you're old if you want to be authentic," I screamed one night when I was typing and doing a lot of the writing on his first and last college term paper. That made him as mad as I've ever seen him. I didn't know then, when we were talking about all the "authentic" crap and typing the term paper, that our whole post-sweetheart life in the little shingled house was a big fat lie, that our little sit-com life and baby-waiting-to-be-born were killing Phyllis, who had been my friend. He got a C minus on that paper. I should say I got a C minus on the paper since I wrote it.

"Do you know what Richie's first words were?" Douglas Smathers does not seem surprised to hear the question asked in the chilled darkness.

"What were they?"

"Slow down, dammit."

Douglas wants an explanation. So I explain. "Richie picked it up on our trip to Alaska. We had to see for ourselves, I guess, if it was really there. Just because the map says so doesn't mean it's true, said Rich. He kept his eyes on the baby most of the way, his head turned away from the highway, which was sometimes just gravel, going seventy, me screaming 'Slow down, dammit,' the baby laughing and finally saying his first words. 'Slow down, dammit.' The only thing that would have made Rich happier just then might have been to hear Richie say out of the blue, 'Speed up, dammit.' "

Douglas laughs, but a serious laugh. I hear myself telling about how I drove myself to the hospital when Andrew was born.

"Rich and Richie were camping out—it was early December—Andrew was born on the eighth. A four-year-old and a so-called grown man out camping at Blowing Rock, that's in the mountains, and the coldest, oldest ones in America, and me about to deliver. 'You can't go,' I cried, then screamed, then fainted. Rich got that look on his face, the one I call crazy, and left for Blowing Rock. You can't plan a divorce on the way to the hospital to have a baby. The boys have never felt one thing against their father, and I know I'm crazy to blame them for loving their father. Andrew, I think, began loving Rich when he was not even born, and Richie, the most high-spirited four-year-old that ever walked, loved him, if it's true about reincarnation, centuries before."

"They stay with *you*, Ruth, though, so that tells me a lot."

"If you can call it staying with me, custody, when they have their father come in to cook them meals. I mean they stay with me, but on his terms, on their terms, probably because he tells them to, tells them they should, they have to, but not to worry about it, he'll be close by, he'll help them see it through. The puppies are probably a bribe to get them to settle down to finishing the third and seventh grades. In fact, Rich was in on the deal to get me to go out on this date with you. I'm sure that he said something like 'Get your mom out of the house and I'll bring toys in for the puppies.' I know that's how it went. Don't even ask about court orders, injunctions. They are like the map of Alaska, a nice piece of paper that doesn't mean a damn thing."

The night walk, the star man's little talk about star frost, the costumes, make me think out loud about Rich to my date. Anyway, he doesn't seem eager to talk and seems happy to listen to me. Until recently with Grace, and now with my date, I have never talked so much, except to paid counselors, about Rich.

When we get to the apartment, I put Elder and Home on their leashes, not that they know what leashes are, and we turn around to walk back to school to get Richie and Andrew. The dogs drag me down the sidewalk. Douglas helps hold them. We are back in the school yard in less than fifteen minutes. Running behind the dogs cheers me up a little; it's like bird watching, only it's dark and the dogs are noisy.

I don't feel my usual half-assed divorced/undivorced self. I feel the way I imagine Dr. Grace Towle must feel.

Thinking about my past makes me sad, but it is nice to have a date and nice in a horrible way to talk about it all.

I begin whistling Mama's favorite song, "Beautiful Dreamer." The vapor comes out of my lips in a thin cylinder of smoking dry ice. I rub my tears off my face with my convenient hair. Douglas says his aunt loved that old song.

The school is dark. The parking lot has one car—my pumpkin-colored Toyota. I check my watch. It is ten fifty-eight. There had been a huge mess to clean up—booths, spilled water from the apple-bobbing tub. Richie had helped with the stage props and the set, which looked like a typical street corner in the United States. Maple Corners, it was called. Ms. Vincent, who loved him for his "dramatic flair" and "gift of the poetic," had let him design it.

The school is locked. We go around to the back entrance to the auditorium. I go around twice. I drop Elder's and Home's leashes, hoping they will find the boys. They make wide arcs over the street in front of the school. It is empty. So are the side streets.

Now, I am crying, without hiding it from my date. I fan my little flashlight high up into the trees lining the sidewalk in front of the school, the ones with the lacy tablecloths and curtains draped over them. I know the boys have gone away with Rich.

God, maybe to Alaska. I feel it somewhere inside me like the beginnings of flu.

Now, in the empty school yard, I hear Richie's raps in my ears. "Let your children go" had been his coded message to me. As soon as I saw the big tree I had known it was Rich but had refused to do anything about it, not that I would have known what to do. He had sat behind me, just waiting to kidnap Richie and Andrew. It was his idea of family life. He had come to the program, dressed up according to the directions in the letter, which the boys must have given him. I never had seen the letter. Not me. He had probably brought nutritional snacks for them.

"He's taken the boys," I scream at the frozen moon, which looked like a prop made out of yellow construction paper. I turn to Douglas. "The boys are kidnapped, driving seventy miles an hour toward Alaska."

"Should I call Ms. Vincent and Ms. Sowers?" Douglas asks me.

"No, the three of them are all too smart for Ms. Vincent and Ms.

Sowers. For you. For me, too. But sure, I'll call them. I saw The Wrench's mom, Dr. Perfect, leave early to get home to report to him on the program, so I know he isn't involved, which is a relief, I guess."

The moon is getting brighter and there are no shadows in the empty school yard.

VI

$\mathcal{I}$ am used to waiting. Waiting for Rich to notice me when I was twelve. After I was fourteen, waiting for my period so I'd know I wasn't pregnant another month. Waiting for Richie to be born. Waiting by myself for Andrew to be born. Waiting for Rich to come home. Waiting for Rich to find where we had moved.

Now I have a date to wait with—for my kidnapped children to come home or call. I don't know or care if a date makes things better. Douglas Smathers doesn't look like a date. He looks like a nice cousin or something, maybe a visiting expert on the devaluation of the dollar. A man who knows a lot but is waiting, waiting for the right time to begin his explanations and discussions. I begin to feel a companionableness in my misery. I check the chest of drawers and see that the boys' best sweats are missing. The blue Duke sets. Douglas is on the phone calling Ms. Vincent and Ms. Sowers and other parents he has met in his workshops on drugs. No one knows anything. He calls Dr. Towle. Seems he knows her from his work in the school. In some ways, he seems a lot like her. He acts as if he knows what to do, what should be done. Who cares. Someday, when we are all old, I'll ask them both to dinner with Ms. Sowers and Ms. Vincent.

Working with old people, I have to wait more than anything else. Waiting is ninety percent of the job. Getting up from a chair takes goldie-oldies five times longer than younger people, ditto for eating— those who can feed themselves. Putting on shoes—those who remember how and have the muscles to bend over. Taking a pill—those who don't have to have it slipped down their throats.

Thelma White makes looking out the window seem like it's being done under water. She repeats all day long, "What time is it?" Telling her the time gives her no comfort. Now I know what she means. I tell Douglas about Thelma.

The longest wait at Elder Home is for the baths—undressing, hoisting them in slings, swinging, soaping, rinsing, drying, dressing. I begin explaining bathing old people. My date asks intelligent questions. I sound like a geriatrics expert conducting a workshop, but I am feeling a sort of out-of-body expertise.

Then I launch into telling him about my dream career, designing clothes for the ancients of the world. Unisex shifts they can slip on easily, instead of dislocating their shoulders and wrenching their spines to find sleeves. These clothes would float toward the old person with bows or ties or scarves all pre-tied, fake buttons, and Velcro fasteners at the back. Perfect for wheelchair life. Perfect for bedridden life.

All these designs are in my head, not on paper yet, and as I describe them, the questions Douglas asks in a very sincere and intelligent way make me think he has some old people in his life. The terrible waiting goes on, but it is filled with questions and answers.

I learn that my date grew up with old people. It seems his grandparents, both sets, lived with him, an only child, all his childhood. He loves old people, actually, more than other people, feels better around them. Of course, he knows that I have seen old people at their worst, and he feels that maybe, yes, he thinks, almost definitely, he has seen old people at their best. His grandfather Smathers was a botanist and his grandfather Whitlow was a carpenter, so whenever PaPa Smathers wanted a greenhouse extension, he only had to mention it to Grandpa Whitlow, who would begin hammering and sawing at once. The two grandmothers ran the house; happily, one did the cooking, the other everything else. They all read together, never had a television, never wanted one. Are they real? Is Douglas? Or did I dream him up to take the edge off in the middle of my nightmare?

"What foreign country was this you lived in with all these active, sweet old people?" I am carrying on my one percent of the conversation at this point with my eyes closed.

"Right here, the good old States, Indiana, as a matter of fact, but I admit it was an unusual way to grow up. My parents had the freedom to develop careers because they had my grandparents to fall back on, to take me off their minds. My mother painted, landscapes. Dad ran a hospital. Nothing spectacular, but all very congenial. Good for me, too, don't you think?" Here the man flexes his muscles like a lifeguard and laughs. It would have been funny, not very, but a little, if it hadn't been for the situation.

I manage then to say I cannot even imagine such a family. Then I add that I have a brother and mother in Illinois, which is somewhere near, I think, Indiana. Douglas laughs and changes the subject. He asks me if I have ever made one of my "old" dresses.

"I did make an outfit for Dorothy Rose Gibbons. She loved it and could manage getting in and out of it herself. There are back opening dresses and slacks on the market, but nothing like what I want to make. Nothing like the mere slips of soft, washable, non-wrinkle, cool, and silky outfits I want to make."

My nice date from a happy childhood says he hopes that I can have my career some day. Maybe a catalog of my outfits will go out all over the country, to Indiana and Illinois and beyond.

I feel encouraged to tell him about my most recent scheme. Last week I dreamed up a new class called Real Life Aerobics. Instead of going to a class, a woman would get a letter telling her that she had already done her week's aerobics if she had done one of the following activities: washed the car, changed the sheets, vacuumed, ironed for an hour, washed three windows, washed dishes five times, or done three loads of laundry. Extra points for going to work, extra points for having a difficult supervisor, extra points for having a conference with a teacher. But the most points, bonus points, are given for waiting for kids. The calories waiting burns up!

Douglas has read that Benjamin Franklin exercised by going up and down steps to increase his heart rate.

What can a person say about that fact? I say, "You don't mean it." He does, but can't remember where he read it.

By now, Douglas is eating a huge Dagwood sandwich made out of things I didn't know were in the refrigerator. He tries to get me to eat, brings me a fourth of his sandwich cut like a club sandwich and turned up in pyramids. He even has found toothpicks to hold them together. He brings me a napkin and a glass of milk. He reports that I need to lay in some new supplies soon, that he has really had to use his imagination to find sandwich makings. I go on about my aerobics for real life.

"Glowing with pride, the letter receivers would improve in body and mind. My Real Life Aerobics would cost five dollars a month, not the one hundred forty-nine I see advertised for the exercise videos." I can hear my voice rising at the injustice of the world. I get more agitated.

"Golden Age Aerobics, the advanced stage of my program, would give credit for looking out of windows, remembering the names of children, folding a towel—real things."

Yes, I tell Douglas, I have several more ideas for modern single mothers and many for the ancients of the world. But when can I get them going? Then I begin telling Douglas about my boss, Ozone Layer. He laughs at her name. I do my impersonation. "Ruth, take over for me. I am too stressed."

Mrs. Osborne never stops talking about how "stressed" she is, too stressed to help with an activity, too stressed to finish doing the payroll, too stressed to fill in for an aide who didn't show up for work. On Tuesday, I had changed the diapers for three residents on the East Wing and would have gone over to West, except Mrs. Ossified needed me to do the payroll and drive the drivables out for an afternoon's roll through downtown.

Then I describe an outing in the van with my ancient buddies. "Wave at General Lee," Martha Pickett says. They all wave. Monument Avenue goes by in slow motion. We wave at General Lee and J.E.B. Stuart, then at Stonewall. We bow at Fontaine Maury's stone globe and Mary Watkins points out the old three-story houses she used to go to for Christmas parties. We drive past the corner where Mary Chestnut lived and partied and grieved with Varina Davis when her son, four years old, I think, fell out of a third- or fourth-story window in the White House of the Confederacy to his death.

Hours later, Douglas agrees with me that all homes should have rooms, as hospitals do, for people to wait in, to do nothing but wait. If my life is an example—and God, please, make it one-of-a-kind—a waiting room should be written into the building codes of America. Fully equipped waiting rooms with bars, as well as less-traditional cabinets for imported movies with blurred subtitles, a wall module aquarium with slow-swimming fish. Maybe have a few bumper cars with silencers, for the children who are waiting to be rescued from being at home.

We wait all night, my date and I. It is a great way to start my dating life. Douglas sits across from me and waits with me. He seems to know how to wait. He has a pocket chess set. If I weren't half insane I would die laughing at the thought of a man bringing a chess set on a date. All I can manage to say is something about his high hopes for a fun evening. He smiles back and says something about chess giving time a whole new dimension. I say so does kidnapping and he laughs out loud, then takes my hands in his and says he is going to go in the kitchen to fix something else to eat. "Be my guest," I say. "I am," he says simply and goes.

I know it is hopeless. I know there is no point in waiting. I should go to the police, and I would, except I've learned my lesson about that option and know what I would hear. "Look, lady, he's not hurting you or the kids. Without a court order, we don't have the authority. Unless there is property damage. Why don't you just go home and wait a little while."

I am not really waiting. I am despairing, I guess you'd call it, though that's not quite the word because I am acting as if I were at a party. I have double vision, seeing myself as I look to Douglas in the mirroring window, all hair and jeans and a glass of straight gin, and seeing how I look to me, a ragmop prealcoholic, ready for Elder Home and fingerpainting.

I wander around the apartment, touching things, checking the chest of drawers again to see where the Duke sweats should be. I cry into the neck of Elder and Home, who lick off the tears. I can see how dumb I am acting, how irresponsible I must look, how unfit as a mother, but Douglas doesn't say anything. He keeps fixing coffee and his clubby sandwiches, whose makings get weirder and weirder every few hours. I drink gin. He starts making a grocery list of things I need in the kitchen.

"Why not, have another, act dumb as you please, dumb as you are," I mumble, lounging on the sofa like an old-time movie queen, swirling the oily-looking gin in the glass—the ice hadn't melted before I added more gin. I know I should be drinking Perrier like Dr. Towle, or Chinese tea.

I check the boys' clothes for the third time. I feel an insane pride in my good shopping skills, at finding name-brand jeans reduced to half price. Those good buys are gone along with the Duke sweats.

"Gone," I call out to Douglas, knowing he cannot know what I'm talking about. Then I rummage around in the big cardboard shoe boxes in the closet. I ask the boxes, "How about shoes, how many pairs?"

Which is crazier, I wonder, talking to myself or talking to a box or the dogs. Douglas answers me and I don't feel so crazy. "Did they take extra shoes and jeans?"

"High tops, canvas, and Nike Airs. Cost an arm and a leg. Just what they wanted."

"Gone!" He echoes me, then adds, "Shouldn't you reconsider and take this to the authorities, if not the police, then some agency? There is too much at stake here, which you know better than I, of course. Your sons have been, well, kidnapped. I would call the police myself, but I am just your date. You are the one who should call. In this situation. I am simply a person you have met through your sons. I don't have any authority. Any power, really."

"Join the party. They'll come home, maybe in a month, when Rich has had enough authenticity and camping or kayaking or whatever he's dreamed up this time."

I come back into the living room and sink down on the sofa, none too gracefully. Then I get up, and using my shoulder to touch base every now and then on the long hall back down to the boys' room, I stagger toward the tall window.

The moon is shining through the old wavy glass and I can see smears on the glass from the outside.

"That's a dog's nose print." I say, soberly, I hope. Then I fall down on Andrew's bed, which smells like the puppies who climb up beside me.

"If I had gotten them a dog earlier, after Alexi was killed. If I had gotten them a dog." I go on and on until I guess I fall asleep with the dogs there beside me. I don't worry about where Douglas will sleep.

~~~

In my dreams, it's the same old story, only clearer and in color with some new features—a sound track that makes my words ring out clear and cold, a time-zoom lens, and an interpreting device that types out comments on the dream across the bottom of the screen. I've dreamed this dream often since I left Rich. He's the villain and the star in every version of it, and I feel his dangerous spirit fill the apartment.

The dream has a plot, which I understand most dreams don't, but this one does: Daddy gets lost; Rich almost kills me. Daddy is found, and I grow up to marry Rich. It's dumb, but it's exactly what happened, only it took a longer time to happen in real life.

"Daddy's lost." This is the clear message that I, the ten-year-old Ruth, deliver in the dream. Mama uses those words as she drives us down to her sister's for help to find Daddy. The two words— "Daddy's lost"—reduce the afternoon we lived through to something new and different.

At ten, I don't know how exact the words "Daddy's lost" are or how they, just two words, make a chisel out of the afternoon, wedge it into the night and, it's not going too far to say, into my life.

Cringing in the backseat of our black, sloped Pontiac, I ride with Mama and my younger brother, James, to tell the Blair cousins that we can't find Daddy. We need their help to find him.

Earlier, that afternoon, another set of cousins, not as important as the Blairs, not as close, Daddy's side, the Marshalls, come over to sit on the porch, trying to be friendly, especially to Mama, who keeps the iced tea coming. She gets the white enamel dishpans of ice out of the freezer and cracks out chunks of ice with the hatchet she uses to split kindling in the winter.

Blades of ice stick out of the quart-sized tea glasses. Stalks of mint, big as celery, freeze next to the ice. Mama is not talking to Rachel Marshall, oh, no. I don't know why, except on general principles.

Rachel is common, and that is the one thing we are not, Mama says.

Rachel gives all the young people parties in her house, which looks very much like ours—huge and gray, like an elephant on its side. And like our house, it has no central heat and very little electricity. At Rachel's winter parties, when you close your eyes for one of her kissing games, which she plays too, as if she were a young person instead of a woman, you can't tell if you are inside the house or still walking toward the front door. She doesn't let the lack of heat stop her from giving a party.

James and I and the Blairs are grateful as hungry dogs for the parties, even if we do stand around the room like statues except when she jerks one of us out in the room to goosestep around the table. We are dancing. I first dance, if that is what the two children galloping around a freezing room are doing, with Rich in that old gray house.

In the dream there are added dashes of color at Rachel's, a roaring fire (what a laugh) and a few huge velvet cushions heaped up in the corner.

The dream shows Rich and me as childhood sweethearts, wretched and trapped by deceit and new kisses, the frozen glamour of Rachel's party.

Rachel has a bowl of red punch on the dining-room table, plates of cookies, and a record player going, its cord running up to the light over the punch bowl. Then she is teaching us to fox-trot. She gets us to stop our mad galloping. Rich is her partner.

"That's nice," Mama says later. She doesn't mean nice in the usual way. She means there is nothing else to say about Rachel. She is saying all that can be said about such a thing. Fox-trotting? If we are going to fox-trot at Rachel's, we will want to go to the Veteran's Hall dances, and over Mama's dead body . . . We know this. Still, we like learning something we will never use. It is like Mama's Latin—there but unused, there if she ever needs it.

This unhelpful wisdom about learning, the dream makes as clear as ice.

Mothers are filled with unnecessary wisdom, things they can never use with their children. Fathers, though, are different. Kids will listen to them, regardless, and put into action any scheme that comes from a father.

Mama does not have much to say to someone like Rachel, someone who likes to ride around in her old plum-colored Kaiser, who likes to give parties for no reason and for the only people who will come—children. Rachel must have seen something alluring and bad in Rich even as a kid, as everyone did, as I did. I know she "encouraged" us as a couple even then, as children at her parties. Rachel, I remember hearing Mama and her sister Marie Blair saying, "went with sawmill men."

Rachel married Daddy's cousin Bill Marshall, and in this dream she wears a bride's smile and, at one point, a white gown, though she must have been forty-two that summer when Daddy disappeared. At her winter parties, she always wore a green satin sheath and silver stockings.

Occasionally, Rachel and Bill would come to see us out of the blue. Bill knew what Mama's language of the ice hatchet and "that's nice" meant, so they didn't come much. When they did, something always happened.

Bill Marshall and Daddy rig up pulleys in the giant oak trees in front of our house, thread a rope between them, and hoist all the kids up for rope rides. One by one, we swing higher than the upstairs windows of our ramshackle seventeen-room farmhouse. Then they lower us. Sometimes, they just pull us up six feet or so and we push each other in heavy, slow arcs.

In the dream, Rich is there, swinging on the rope, working the pulleys with James. He is, by then, James's hero and mine. Mama never notices him until it is too late, and Rachel has taken over by then, having us come over to her place to play in the creek. Mama doesn't know Rich is there; she thinks it is just James and me with the Marshall cousins, which is bad enough. When she catches on, it is too late, and she never lets Rich back in our house. So from that time until we were seventeen, Rich never came to my house. He came the day we got married—my birthday. That was the second time I saw Mama cry.

Daddy and Bill sit in Bill's Kaiser instead of on the oak tree roots near the pulleys. They turn working the pulleys over to us. One of us rides up while the rest of us grab on and weigh down the ends of the ropes.

Mama won't look up at us, stick figures hanging up in her front yard, like shirts on a clothes line. She is busy carrying the iced tea out to the Kaiser, where Daddy and Bill Marshall are sitting, elbows out the windows, as if they were driving off somewhere. Rachel finally gets in the backseat, as if she wanted to go away with them.

Mama knocks on the car hood, as if it were the door of a house, and then walks back to Daddy's side and says, "Drink this." They take the glasses into the car and when she gets back in the house, they dump the tea out and pour in the whiskey Bill has brought.

I am an expert on whiskey bottles. James and Rich and I know most of Daddy's hiding places—the culvert, the barn, the gully grown over with honeysuckle, the tool box. Sometimes we take the flat bottles to Mama, sometimes we pour out the whiskey if we find them in time. Rich sometimes drinks what is left in the bottles.

Now, without my seeing how she gets there, Rachel is in the kitchen with Mama. I feel sure she wants to take a ride up on the rope. She probably will point her toes or do something fancy for us, hang by one arm. She looks like a girl waiting to go somewhere, for something to happen.

Leave it to Rich to think of letting me hang on the rope up in the air. I think it is Rich's way of having me completely in his power—hanging up high, about to drop to my death.

I can see straight into my bedroom window. My arms are pulling out of their sockets, my feet weigh two tons. I can't scream with my chin crammed down on my chest in the V between my straight-up arms. But worse, my hands are burning through the blood on the rope.

"Let me down, let me down," I always whisper at this point in the dream in a strangled scream.

Daddy and Bill get out of the Kaiser and head for the barn, walking like very old people or babies. I can see them appear under me, then disappear in the direction of the barn.

Automatically, I think "more whiskey," as if I were on the ground and everything were fine, no problem except how to talk to Rachel and Mama in the same day.

That's when Daddy goes off to get lost, but we don't think of it as being lost yet because I'm still on the rope. I have priority, I guess. The dream, though, in its subtitle typed across the bottom of the screen, lets me know up on the rope, hands ripping apart, skin left on the rope if I fall for five hours to the ground, that Daddy is getting himself lost. Not Bill Marshall—he is going to be fine, going home to the nice old gray house with Rachel.

In the summer, our houses are mansions. The breezes blow through them from the river.

James and his Marshall buddies, Driscoll and Parker, work the pulleys under Rich's direction. As usual, Rich is giving orders, laughing. Then Rich gets the pulleys locked up somehow. On purpose. I know he is to blame. The words typed across the picture of me swinging gently in the air say he's to blame.

I hang there until Mama happens to come out the door with more iced tea. She drops the pitcher and I hear a long crack on the porch. I see a brown-and-white hawk wheel out of sight in the blue sky, which looks like the afterlife. We don't use "heaven" and "hell" in my family, except as exclamations.

That's what I'll sound like when I hit, I think, a long wet splat. I can think while hanging on the rope, I just can't yell or even talk.

Mama is running—I can hear her. Then I can see her run toward the pulley on one oak tree, but I can't turn my head, it is so crammed down between my arms.

Then she runs to the other pulley. I hear her steps echo, the yard is baked so hard. Splat, splat, I keep thinking. It hasn't rained in six weeks. The dream is factual about the ground, the hawk, and the sky.

Rain is what Rachel tried to talk to Mama about when they first got there. Mama hates talk about the weather.

Mama and Rachel, the bride, get me down. Rachel looks like an angel-bride with winglike sleeves. She flies up and rides me down. Rich is sitting on the roots of the oak tree, looking up at us as if he had nothing to do with my hanging on a rope.

Then Rachel, maybe in a going-away suit, but still young and a party-lover, gets Bill into the Kaiser and takes him home. Mama never likes Rachel any better after she rescues me, and intuitively blames Rich. The fault is not so clear-cut, because James is also involved, along with the Marshall cousins. Mama is mad at the Marshalls for the whiskey, anyway. She just looks at Rich, a long look. The bride, billowy in her gown, is Rachel, not tough-skinned and scuttling as she is on earth, but sailing up to hold me on the trip to earth so my hands won't pull off at the wrists or knuckles. Her dress is nothing like the blue granny gown I wore to get married in, denim with lace at the neck and bottom. Across the bottom of the dream the words are running together: YOU'LLBESORRY, printed out on the baked ground under the rope.

Six weeks pregnant, in that little house, waiting for Rich to come home, I felt as if I were swinging from the rope.

At our wedding in Gastonia, Rich wore an oxford-cloth shirt like a college boy's, jeans, and boots.

In my sleep, I feel resentful. I feel my headache. WHO, I want to shout back in caps to the words, SOWHODOESN'TKNOWTHAT?

The dream somehow, like the swooping hawk, fills me with a sense of being in a place highly dangerous (up on a rope) but watched by Rich. Smiling Rich.

With the Marshalls gone, me down from the rope, we decide Daddy is lost. Mama stands in the dark yard under the rope and calls, "Ah, Ed, ah, Ed." No answer, so Mama, who has never done the least thing that can pass for dramatic, never cried, even sighed for effect, goes—for her—crazy. "Get in the car. Your daddy's lost." Then she keeps saying "lost" driving down to her sister's.

When we get to the Blair place, I have to crouch down and lean hard to bang open the door of the car, hang my right leg out to be snagged as Mama tries to get the motor to cut off. It coughs, refuses to die, but I have already hit the hard ground running backward, slamming the door, then turning to rush through the dark warm rain, which started after the Marshalls left, into my cousin's house.

I am racing to beat James with the news that we have lost Daddy. As it turns out, Rich somehow beats us both and gets to say what I am planning to say.

"Their daddy's lost," he announces. He is as solemn as it is possible for him to be, but he knows he is lucky to find himself in the middle of a manhunt, so he repeats the phrase in his dark voice, which he had even then. James and I can hear Rich as we are running from the car up the porch steps behind him. So by the time we get to the living room, where the Blair cousins are propped on the sofa, and one to each of the easy chairs, one flat on the floor, Rich has stolen our thunder about being almost orphaned, close to being orphans, about losing our father.

The Blairs look at us, not surprised to hear something crazy. Maybe a little surprised that my father, a man forty-three years old with wire-rim glasses, who sharpens wood saws, is lost. Definitely surprised to hear me repeat "Daddy's lost." There is nowhere to be lost. Lost? Around here? This is the good news. A lost man is news. I can feel attention turn and fix on me. I hold up my hands, which Mama has bandaged in strips of an old sheet with little shavings of butter on the rope burns. I can tell the bandaged hands do not go with the message, but so what, they go with the whole story, and I keep holding them up.

Uncle Ed Marshall, a lost man! In a way, he is probably the only man in the county who could have gotten himself lost. I am not the only one in the room who believes the report. My brother, James, does, of course, but that is because he wants to be the one to report to the Blairs, which he does, but three minutes after Rich does.

"My daddy's lost." By now James is standing at the door and facing the Blairs in their evening slump around the room, radio on full blast, week-old funny papers wide open, boots sitting under the wood stove as if it were February instead of June, cooking to a hard-glazed ceramic finish. The smell of wet leather and mud seems to be steaming straight up. The Blairs always wear boots in case they have an adventure to embark on—they think like that, something like the way Rich does.

In those three minutes, I move across the room to the Blairs and wedge myself onto the sofa between my cousins Pete and Tom.

I begin thinking like a Blair, just as I always do when I am with them. Most of the time their first words are "What in the hell are you talking about? Let's get this straight now." I am thinking right along with them, "Lost? What, around here? What on earth are you saying! Then, well, let's move it, get on our boots and go find crazy, drunk Ed, who can't be lost around here."

Rich volunteers to lead the search party. Tom, my oldest cousin, reaches across his blue plaid chest to cut the radio off right in the middle of his favorite old song about a dying man who is crawling across a desert looking for water. Tom loves the part about mirages.

In the sudden quiet, I hear Mama saying "Ed's gone" to her sister in the kitchen.

"Gone?" My aunt Marie lets hope singe her question.

"I don't mean he's dead. I mean gone. No, he's off somewhere, probably on the place, and I want to ask the boys to go get him."

"When did he go?"

"Just a little while ago."

We are listening hard in the living room. What does Mama mean by saying it wrong, that Daddy is gone when he is lost. We are forming a search party in a few minutes. Being lost is something no one has ever been. Gone means he is coming back. Lost means we'll stand at the edge of the woods and wave flashlights and yell; then we'll fan out into the woods and never find him, or maybe find him dead. I wish our dogs knew how to hold their heads down and run crooked.

Mama repeats "gone" several more times. Then she says she thinks Ed is lost. Dumb me, I believe her.

This rope thing is maybe the last straw. She tells Aunt Marie about the time Daddy taught us to drive.

Mama did not like Daddy's way with us, with children, and I must say I never felt much like a child, and of course it has occurred to me that Rich took over in my life (I am not unaware of the big reason I fell for Rich) where Daddy left off. To teach me to drive he put James and me in the car and drove out to the big field behind the house, put the car in second gear, got out and slammed the door and said, "Now you two can learn to drive." We drove around and around the field until Mama caught us. I was six and James was four. Mama ran alongside the car, talking to me through the rolled-up window. "Turn the key off," she kept yelling. I didn't know how.

Finally, she got into the car and drove us back to the house.

I will always love driving and feel its dangers. I wish my dream about swinging on the rope had typed out that I should have become an astronaut, at least a pilot, given my formative experiences. But now it seems obvious to me that I became Rich's wife in place of becoming an astronaut.

Working with old people is not the career that should have grown out of my childhood. It's so quiet—not what a person who hung from a rope, then married her hanger, whose father enjoyed being lost, would choose. "Choice" is a fantasy word, a dream word, I think. But I want to stop being a rope hanger. I want to work with old people, who aren't all that quiet, anyway, when you get to know them.

How do we find Daddy? It takes some doing. Because it is dark, because it is raining, because the Blairs get into the act, we end up with a woods full of people, especially the bunch of alcoholics, all searching for my daddy.

Aunt Marie had decided to call the alcoholic center, the farm that turned into a precursor of the Betty Ford place. I guess Mama could not stop her. I know that Mama always thought it was the nearest nothing kind of treatment to have alcoholics play softball, which is what they did on the Jones place. It was renamed Creekwood Treatment Center, and all we knew of it was that the alcoholics played ball in spring, winter, fall, summer—all year round. Daddy never set foot on the place. He did not "have a problem." Anyway, Aunt Marie must have gone to the phone and called Creekwood.

Rich rides along with the alcoholics—more danger, more chance of a wreck or an escape.

Later, when Rich would get drunk, he would say he was feeling fine, just fine, he was a little high. His lips gave him away. They would thicken, and look South American instead of North Carolinian.

Once in High Point, when he was looking up at me from where he had fallen through the Sheetrock floor of the attic of the old house we were renting (six weeks in that place), he laughed and said, "Now, I've lived out the rope thing, and you've paid me back for getting you hung up in the air, Rue. You've gotten your revenge."

"Fine," I screamed. "Sure, you have paid me back, but not with this little fall through the ceiling. You're not hurt, you're fine. Your neck's not broken."

This was two years after our Gastonia runaway wedding. Andrew wasn't born. We were not having any more babies, a decision the human race makes after the first baby.

We were fighting all the time, even over childhood events like the rope. Rich had been exploring the attic of the old house and walked on what he thought was the attic floor. It was only the ceiling of the upstairs bedroom. Crashing through the joists, he scared Richie and me almost to death. With blood running out of his nose as he talked, he explained to Richie, a two-year-old, that it was faster to fall than to take the ladder. Either way, though, Richie's father, yes sir, would get himself back to his son. Richie nodded his head like a very old man, drinking in his words. Unborn, unconceived Andrew agreed.

The next week Rich went to South America. He knew someone who knew someone who said he could come live there for a while. He stayed three months. When he came home, after a while, we had Andrew. When Andrew was two, I couldn't take any more.

The Blairs get their boots on. The vanload of alcoholics arrive, singing, of all things, "Ninety-nine bottles of beer on the wall." Mama keeps saying "lost." The van follows us back home. I confuse Rich's drunk driving when we were married with this scene in the dream of losing Daddy. Rich used to drive with his lights out, drunk as anything.

We all seem sure of one thing: Daddy has gotten himself lost at home somewhere. And he is, really. It takes maybe forty-five minutes to find him, dry and warm in the barn, back behind the old 1932 Mack truck he was going to restore. Sleeping "like a baby," the leader of the alcoholics says, in a voice like a doctor's.

The Blairs get all mixed in with the men from Creekwood and I don't think they like not being the leaders of the expedition, but by then it is out of our hands. I don't think we'd eaten that day. I walk behind the alcoholics, but when I hear the leader say "like a baby," I run back to the house and like a crazy thing, a squirrel maybe, get under my bed and hide until everyone has gone away—alcoholics and Blairs and Rich.

Coming downstairs in one neat jump, I want to unwrap my hands to see if they have stopped bleeding. Mama is telling Daddy he is lost. Then she falls down and hits the floor with a loud noise, like the one I almost made from the rope. Daddy doesn't go to pick her up.

He looks the way he did when he rolled the wheelbarrow over to offer me a ride after I fell off Beauty. James and I go over and say in our best voices, "Get up, Mama. Can you get up?"

She says yes she can, and the dream typewriter obligingly types YOU'LLBESORRY under the picture of her crumpled on the floor. Then again, the words flash on in the dumb obvious caps the same message: YOU'LLBESORRY.

~~~

I hear Douglas trying to be quiet fixing something else in the kitchen. The sun has replaced the moon in the window. It is a century later, the next day, the first of November. On my first grown-up date, I have let a man spend the night with me. So what if it's on unusual terms, it's still true. So what if I slept with the dogs and I don't know where or if he slept.

Then I smell toast beginning to burn, that sharp smokey smell that always made me happy as a girl. Mama burned toast regularly, although she would run to the oven every morning surprised to see she had done it again. We always laughed at her and came to like nice black toast. A new day, burning toast, we always felt good in the mornings, no matter what had happened the day before. I can remember that good morning feeling, crisp, sharp. And one good thing is happening: I am remembering that I do know a good policeman, state trooper, whatever. Officer something eleven . . . 711. Officer Arm something, Armstrong, no, Armenfish, Armentrout! "Armentrout, Officer 711," I say to myself, in a professional if exhausted tone, as if I had been performing brain surgery all night. I will explain who Officer 711 is to Douglas after I call from Andrew's phone.

The dispatcher says she's sorry, but 711 is not on duty. It's his vacation week. Could I leave a message?

My head is full of hot rolling oils. My heart is grinding around against my ribs. I try to sit up but the sunlight pushes me back down. It's Saturday. Soccer? Saturday inspection? No, none of the above.

I don't have any children to yell at to get ready. They are gone.

VII

*W*hen the puppies bark, they could wake up the Confederate soldiers at the Petersburg Crater. They tune up with growls, then almost sing, every morning starting any time from three on. When I don't get up and take them downstairs, I pay later. I put a big litter box out on the roof, but I am afraid to get out there with them at night. Most of the time, I force myself to get out of bed at three to take them down to the street.

On those trips down the stairs, I'm herded as if I were in front of a small army, driven along by soft thundering forces. Eight big feet hitting the steps between my bare ones. I hang on to the banister.

The roof litter box may have been safer. There is no light on the stairs, for all its hand-carved fancy newel post. There is a streetlight that floods the roof.

In the day, I don't have the nerve to get the dogs out on the roof and try to train them to use the litter box with people watching me.

I am horrified with myself for thinking about training dogs when I have lost my children. I listen for the dogs but don't hear anything.

I can't move a muscle, can*not* get out of bed. If I didn't have this date to deal with, this Douglas, who had spent the night in my apartment, I would have stayed there forever, staring at the ceiling. I hear something going on in the kitchen. I am used to Richie and Andrew cooking, making messes and noise, but not a spend-the-night date. First date, blind date. My life is taking off without me. I'm snowballing through hell into the singles scene.

This morning the dogs are quiet, a first. I have heard of dogs dying of broken hearts. Maybe they know the boys have gone and are beginning their decline.

For no reason, I turn toward the phone and punch the star man's number on Andrew's phone, the one Rich gave him. I memorized the number when it was given on his show last night. He wanted calls, he said, questions about his new topic, star clusters. I have wanted to call him for some time. His voice on the radio sounds as if it were coming from a star.

"May I speak to the star man?" I get a bored voice at the radio station. "You can't get Al," it says, "until program time. His home phone is unlisted."

I dread having to talk to Douglas. So I just sit up on the edge of the bed, at least I have gotten that far, in the weak November 1 sunshine, like a cat. A mother cat. I bet she would prowl around looking for her kittens. Smelling the puppies, she, the mother cat, would know they had eaten her babies. Unlike me, she, good cat-mother, would do something.

I could wait for Officer Armentrout to come home from vacation and take pictures of Richie and Andrew down to his headquarters so the milk companies could print them on their cartons. I could take the fingerprints the school had made "in the event of a crime." Kidnapping is a crime, even if it's a parent who drove them away and the kids wanted to go, were thrilled to go, packed up to go. I would have shot Rich if I had a gun and if he were close enough for me to hit and if someone, maybe God or this date cooking away in the kitchen, would clean up the blood and make the body disappear. I am sick of aftermaths, consequences of a minute's worth of feeling good. As the counselor told me, children of alcoholics are addicted to excitement. That's me. Except I'm trying to get over it. Elder Home is not exactly exciting; that's a first step. Certainly, my first date since my divorce is a quiet type. But he's too noisy now, cooking. I will fix him up with Dr. Towle the first chance I get.

I can smell the dogs. But they are still quiet.

I can't go on TV and beg for the return of my children. I know they will come back sooner or later. Richie wouldn't want to stay away too long and hurt his chances for honor roll, even if Andrew would like to stay until he failed the third grade so he could have more conferences with teachers about his adjustment problems.

What is the worst thing, what makes my ribs hurt as if my heart were swelling up and breaking them, is that the boys might get killed doing whatever it is they are doing. Will they be alive when they get back home, I yell down into the pillow, which smells like the goo Andrew puts on his Mohawk strip of hair to make it stand straight up.

Even at his best, Rich could manage to kill them accidentally with his river-jungle way of making decisions. Not even counting the drive to Alaska, his way with the boys is dangerous. His idea of playing with babies was to throw Richie high in the air, or to hold Andrew over his head on the palm of one hand and run at full speed.

By now, I'm in the kitchen drinking the strong coffee my date has made and telling him how Rich played with the boys when they were babies. The worst time was with Andrew. He was fourteen months old, just walking. He loved to push the kitchen chairs together, climb up, and walk on them, back and forth, back and forth.

Rich watched him, smiling all the time, then pulled a chair out of the lineup just as Andrew was stepping toward it, big fat baby foot high and crookedly aimed at the cool vinyl seat of the red chair. He fell, his chin hitting the seat of the chair, jamming his teeth into his gums, hitting his head on the metal rim of the table and then on the floor. I couldn't believe what I was seeing.

Douglas asks what Rich did when he saw the baby bleeding.

Oh, Rich picked him up, but without any acknowledgment of his part in causing the blood running out of Andrew's mouth or the long ridge rising on his head. Later that night, Andrew's chest turned black and blue. Still, Rich did not say a word, a normal word, like "sorry" or "my fault," much less something like "I don't know what got into me."

Telling Douglas about Andrew and the chairs makes me jump up out of the kitchen chairs as if I were not me but an athlete. I jog to the bathroom. I can walk as perfectly as a cat, a mother cat. It's a miracle, a star-cluster miracle. I am investigating, on the prowl. I feel better. A little bit, anyway.

My head stops splitting open and swelling up to accommodate my infected brain. I look in the medicine cabinet for the gel Andrew uses. I hear my date in the kitchen frying something.

"It's gone," I yell to the dogs and Douglas. "Andrew's hair gunk is gone."

"With him," I add to the frightening person in the mirror, who looks capable of kidnapping children or even murdering them.

The dogs run in to see what I'm doing. They look normal and curious. I hold on to the sink, then think I better move over to the commode, where the gin from last night and the cup of coffee in my stomach turn to green gasoline, then come up and out, a fountain of acid. Elder and Home sniff and whimper, and flop down on the old-fashioned stone-tiled bathroom floor. They are as black as the black tiles.

"That's better," I groan at them. "I can get started now." A new day, the first day of the rest of my life. Brushing my teeth and scrubbing the headache out of my forehead with a washcloth, I refuse to look in the mirror again.

I hear the phone ring. My date answers it.

Great, it's probably Ozone Layer wanting me to come to work today. She would think kidnapping was a good way to handle babysitting. She won't be surprised that I have a man here early in the morning.

Then I realize it could be Andrew or Richie, and I jerk my arm out of the socket before I have sense enough to unlock the door.

Douglas hands the phone over his shoulder. It is Andrew.

"Where are you? Come home, this minute. I want you and Richie home. Now. Put Richie on the phone."

"He's in the bathhouse, Mama. I'll tell him you wanted to talk to him."

"What bathhouse?"

"The one here. It's up the hill from our tent. On a trail and everything, definitely neat."

"You tell me where you are now. And put your father on the phone. Now."

"I can't, Mom. He went to get more change in case you wanted to talk a long time. He said to tell you we were fine. And we are. We weren't cold and we cooked over the fire this morning already. Today, we want to climb a mountain. We may see some otters."

A recorded voice, that familiar computerized phone voice, breaks in and cuts into Andrew's "Gotta go." The line goes dead and I slide down to the floor. I remember that the boys have fallen in love with mountains lately. They want to ski and live in a mountain cabin. Richie has volunteered to start an Alpine Club at school. He's been reading about rock climbing and spelunking. Elder and Home lick my hands. I know I must stand up and take them downstairs.

The boys are alive. At a state park in the mountains. It could be hills, with a bathhouse, a campground.

When I say otters to Douglas he says that will give us a hint. We need a map of state parks, he thinks. Right, I say, just what I keep on hand.

I should have moved three months ago, to Kansas or Utah, where there are plenty of old people. I should have left this old house converted into apartments that have windows looking out on roofs where ex-husbands can camp out with a dog. I cry all this to Douglas, who puts his arms around me and pats my hair.

I remember I do have an old map of the state, the one I use to keep us on the move. It is soft with age. I have traced all our moves in black Magic Marker. Around Richmond, there are black zigzags.

"Peaks of Otter," Douglas mutters, explaining to me and the dogs. "They're at the Peaks. It's about three hours from here." That's where Ozone Layer took the Elder Home residents last month to see the foliage. She takes all the good trips. I had wanted to go and take Andrew and Richie because of their new alpine interests. Richie's relief map he made out of flour and oatmeal is around here someplace, I tell Douglas. In fact, I bet they told Rich how disappointed they were to miss the Elder Home trip, so he said they didn't have to worry about mountains. No problem. Then he planned this little field trip. Andrew had thought he would see a real otter if he got to go.

"I'll get dressed; then I am calling the ranger station. Some park ranger may remember a van with two boys and a crazy man." I am talking to myself and to Douglas, who stops hugging me to read the map and now has turned the eggs over and started toast. He comments again on the gaps in my kitchen supplies, saying he guesses the boys packed up some food to take. I take a look in the cabinets, and now it comes to me that Andrew had put in a lot of special requests on the last trip to the grocery store. Hamburger, extra lean. Ranch chips, Sloppy Joe mix, pickles.

I forget that I am already dressed. I never undressed. I'm slipping toward Alzheimers. When you don't know if you're dressed or not, that's an early sign. I get a number at a ranger station and talk to a military-sounding man who says he did see a party of three with a big dog go toward the highest campsite.

"I don't know how long it will take to drive up there," I say to the ranger, who tells me it's three hours from Richmond.

The dogs look as if they know everything but are interested in hearing it again. After I hang up, I feel that I must call right back and explain that the boys are mine, that they have been more or less kidnapped. When I call back, I get a machine. The ranger must have clicked it on right after he talked to me.

"No answer at the ranger station. Just a machine. I left a message that I was on my way. I made up something that would not be alarming, that would make the ranger feel some concern, I hope. I said their father forgot the older son's medicine and that I had to find him to give it to him, that it could upset his metabolism not to have it. Ritalin."

Douglas is fixing me some kind of egg mac-sandwich, which I think will make me throw up again, but I eat it anyway to be polite, even under these circumstances. I answer his unspoken question. "No, you can't go with me." He starts to insist, but when he sees I'm shaking, he lets it go.

Maybe my children have drowned in a river or choked on a jungle vine or been bitten by a jungle snake by now.

~~~

So, I drive toward the mountains to find my children and their kid-napper—their father, my childhood sweetheart. My car has four new tires. That's some comfort.

I feel vomit edging up into my mouth. The egg sandwich holds it down.

I remember Richie saying vomiting is called "shouting Ralph" and

I do feel like yelling, "Ralph, Ralph" out the window. The car smells of the coffee Douglas handed me.

Like so many things in my life, this trip to the mountains is the opposite of what it was supposed to be, what a trip to the autumn mountains is for other people. They go to see the foliage, in happy circumstances. They have husbands who sell insurance. They have children who are practicing corner shots for the soccer game. Grace Towle has a kid home in bed with an asthma attack. She's lucky. She knows where The Wrench is.

Other people would have a plaid wool blanket with long fringes, a thermos of perked coffee, hiking boots, long underwear. A hamper in the trunk with long loaves of French bread, real butter, and radishes and scallions to slice on the buttered bread. Deli meats in lopsided stacks. Richie had read about French picnics for a social studies project—that's where the idea of onions and radishes, butter and long loaves came from as I drove west to find my kidnapped, not dead, I prayed, children.

I think of my father's funeral, on another November day, a brilliant blue, the brown oak leaves still on the trees. I wondered then what a normal funeral would be like. To bury a normal father, one who taught you to drive the regular way, not by putting you in a running car out in a field. Not a drunk man who was lost most of the time, one way or another. Everyone kept saying that the beautiful weather on the day of the funeral was a help to us. Maybe it was. Maybe it is some help on my trip to find Andrew and Richie that I don't have to use the windshield wipers and don't have a flat tire.

"Read about the heavens declaring," my mother had said to the young minister, who had never met Daddy and wanted to do his funeral service about fathers and children. "No, no. The heavens declaring would suit us better," Mama said in her absolute voice.

I drive the back roads toward the mountains. I panic on the interstates. The trucks make me paranoid, and once some drunk boys played bumper tag with me on I-85. I'll make better time and keep from losing my mind, what's left of it, if I drive west on old Route 60.

I keep my eyes on the sides of the road, watching for hidden state troopers. Maybe Officer Armentrout will appear with Dr. Alonzo Johnson, who is escaping, kidnapped by 711, in plain clothes, vacation clothes, to help me. They get their salaries, I've heard, plus a little on the side from the judges, in the counties. WELCOME TO POWHATAN. A slate sign. Then Cumberland County announces itself. I turn at Hillcrest on Route 45 to Farmville, then take 460 to Lynchburg, around Appomattox.

My head is so bad I stop for coffee. I remember General Grant had a migraine in Farmville just before Appomattox.

Richie packed up everything to take with him. Packing up what he calls supplies, even if it's just to walk to soccer practice, is one of his talents. He organizes backpacks of food, "in case," he always says, and never finishes the sentence.

It makes me mad, on top of being scared to death that they are dead, to think of the three of them planning what food they could take from my kitchen.

If they haven't already fallen into a ravine from a rope Rich has rigged up from one Peak of Otter to another, if they *are* there at the Peaks safe and sound, I will be mad as hell.

I am crying again and my head is swelling again. But the egg sandwich stays down. My nice date left after he put me in my car and gave me the coffee and his number to call when I knew anything about the boys. He would feed the dogs and take them out for a walk later, he said. He would call our friends, Grace Towle and The Wrench.

I remember Andrew's first day of school. He came running up the steps, shouting "I'm me, Mama, I'm me. I'm not Richie. I'm me." He had thought, until the day he went to school and the teacher gave him his name tag, that he was part of Richie, like an arm or leg.

I swing off at the sign for the Peaks of Otter. The fast-food places have dried up on the highway. The boys may be waiting to die, bleeding under a rock, Rich looking down at them as if he had nothing to do with it.

I stop at the ranger cabin.

"I called ahead. The ranger, maybe it was you, said he had seen a party of three, and a big black dog, going toward the highest campsite."

The ranger is soft and pink, not what I expected from his voice. He waves me on. I drive fast. The cold coffee makes me forget that my head and ribs hurt.

At the second entrance to the park, I stop and go to find the second ranger. He is leaning on the wooden display counter filled with Indian arrowheads and hatchets.

"Bringing the medicine to your son?" He smiles a nice official smile. "I got a call from Station One that you were coming."

"Yes. Could you point me in the right direction?"

I park across the lot from an old yellow VW van. Rich's. I walk over to it, and through the window I see a bag of dog food and some of Andrew's figures, his doll babies, the ones he fills his pockets with, for his space games, so when he's trapped in some adult place, like the dentist's office or with me at Elder Home, he can play.

I come back to the ranger and mention the Ritalin that I must take to my son, whose father forgot to pack it. We seem to be two professionals at work. I sound like this at Elder Home and am pleased with the professional voice I use with the ranger. I sound like a colleague of Dr. Towle's.

"Take the Apennine Way to the first turnoff, then climb to the Nepal station; it's a tough climb, and I hope you have the right shoes for it. I'm sorry you can't drive on up, but we've had rock slides this week, showers of rock, really. No vehicles allowed." He looks down at my Reeboks with the blue leather piping.

I start up the mountain, wishing I had a gun. I get into a steady, swinging climb; I charge ahead and then have to lean on a tree. It's a trail designed for people like me who are not in shape. Steps set into some of the steeper places, little signs telling the elevation and famous disasters, and sometimes a bench. But the benches (six in all) are always full of foliage viewers. I must look like what I am not—healthy, a grain eater, strong.

At 4:07 I am at the plateau for the campsite called Everest. It juts out into the sky.

What now? What can I do? Make a citizen's arrest of my own children and their father? It is already dark near the trees, though the sun is washing the plateau.

"Climb more," I say out loud. "I may have to be helicoptered down, but I'm going up to their tent and get a few things straight." Then I add to the air in the valley stretched below me, "If I felt any worse, I'd be dead." Daddy used to say that in the mornings and I know at last exactly what he meant.

111

VIII

I can't die, much as I want to. I have to climb a goddamned mountain to find my babies.

When I go crazy I think of Richie and Andrew as babies, a thought that almost immediately drives me crazier. Maybe the word "baby" makes everyone relax a minute, but those who know babies, after that one minute of sweetness and calm, tense up as if a radio had been dropped into their bathtub.

I think of the little rabbitlike movements they made, inside me and after they were born—the little thumpings that say, "Help, help me. I can't live more than an hour or so without you, you big clumsy thing." The voltage hits me, after the first thought.

To think of my babies up on a mountain with a man who thought that either a river or a jungle would be a fine way home, that a Phyllis or a Ruth would do okay to have a baby with, whichever, either was good, is too much for me.

Andrew and Richie are harder to live with at eight and twelve than they were as babies, much worse than thumpers and wavers. As babies they were right there in my hands, in my sight, to feed or kiss holes in their faces, change or bathe.

But I can still feel the thumping, like tom-toms, from far away up the mountain calling, "Help us, help us."

Tall and strong boys, Andrew and Richie—my babies—were calling long-distance, packing up supplies, arranging to be kidnapped, getting me a date. They did it all, except drive.

And for all I knew, they had driven up here to the Peaks of Otter while Rich sat in the back drinking his six packs. Maybe he lay down in the back and left the driving entirely to Richie. Andrew probably picked out the tapes for them, riding shotgun while Richie hung his left arm out the window, driving with his right paw stuck on the steering wheel, like Rich. Anything was possible, even a twelve-year-old at the wheel, kidnapping his brother and himself.

I used to think the way Rich drove was sexy. All the sexy habits of Southern men in their cars or trucks I can see budding in Richie—slouching against a car door, fiddling with the radio, shifting in the seat, spitting his tobacco juice into the beer can, hunching forward and grinning into the side mirror to pass somebody on the right-hand side, lane or no lane.

History might repeat itself, but I would be dead, I hoped, and wouldn't have to look at Richie or Andrew turned into a Rich. Yes, they probably had the windows down barreling across Virginia. Speakers blaring, racing with the wind, riding the highways to the mountains. I knew they were happy.

I am about to fall down again from thinking.

I can smell the campfires. I must be close to them.

Some fires cup their fingers at me. I stop, sliding down on my knees. The leaves fly up and I can see a campfire up the trail. The tent sites spread out over the top of the mountain, three or four red fires. Which one is my fire?

Another fifty yards takes me up, near the dark sky.

Without feeling my legs working, I somehow get to the first fire. Two old people are busying themselves in slow motion around it. They look like escapees from Elder Home. Maybe they were left by Ozone Layer, like Eskimos left on a piece of ice to die, happy.

Yes, they have seen a man with a beard and two fine-looking boys—one looked like an Indian, his haircut—and a big black dog they called Dover. About ten minutes ago. They had just gotten their

Coleman stove started. Now it is going like forty and they offer me some smoking-hot Brunswick stew.

I can't answer, holding to the tree where I've propped myself to ask them questions. I shake my head, no thank you.

I need to push on, I tell them, because I need to get to one of the boys, take him his medicine.

"He did look sick, very ill, in fact, not the taller one. The tall one kept patting the sick one, telling him he'd be all right in a little while. I am sure the medicine you're bringing will help. What a good mother you are to come up the mountain at dark to bring medicine for your son. I know many of today's young mothers who would say it wouldn't matter one time, to miss taking a medication. But as I said, the little one with the Indian haircut looked very ill."

I leave before the Eskimo lady finishes.

A second fire. It's glowing but has been kicked out, in a hurry. No one there, but all the supplies are scattered. Tent up, bedrolls inside, half-opened bag of marshmallows propped too close to the fire, the ones I bought last week. Rich's camp.

It's dark now and quiet as a mountaintop can be with the wind shrieking.

I scream up into the wind. I call their names. I call Rich. I call my dead, lost daddy. I throw in the star man. Then Douglas Smathers. I call my new friends up into the black wind. Grace Towle, Officer Armentrout, Alonzo Johnson. Then I call Rich's name again. I know I am far gone.

"I forgive you. You didn't mean anything. I will never move again. I am glad we have two dogs."

No answer.

It is dark and cold, "seriously dark and cold." Andrew loves the word "seriously." It's the opposite of the weather at the end of my rope dream, when it was damp and warm. But it's frightening in the same way, except worse.

Losing a father is easier than losing children. I am thinking in simple blocks, like a baby's first pyramid of big sponge blocks. Maybe Daddy got lost that time because he couldn't stand James and me or Mama. Compared with a kidnapper, a lost man is a dream of a father. I had a perfect childhood compared with what is happening now.

My poor children—snatched off, even if they helped snatch themselves, almost killed, even if they enjoyed every minute.

I know that Andrew and Richie planned this trip, but I am sure they didn't mean for it to turn out this way. They don't know their father. And the sickness worries me. Andrew is never sick. That's one of The Wrench's fascinations for him—his asthma attacks. Andrew envies them, and I hear him practicing tortured breathing.

They are up here with a man who thinks a dark cold mountain is just fine, as fine as a second-story apartment. Equals. River or jungle.

The word "Andrew" sounds like "And You" when I call to make it last longer against the wind. I hear the name fall away down through the trees.

From the woods comes a woman's voice, a deep Southern movie drawl, answering.

"Honey, those boys tore out of here a little while back. I think the young one was sick. Anyway, the daddy or whoever, was carrying him down the mountain the shortcut to the parking lot and he was moving like Richard Petty on the Charlotte track—he's my boyfriend. No, I'm kidding you, he's not, but I wish he was, and every time I say his name, I add 'he's my boyfriend,' just to see if it'll bring me good luck. But I tell you, those three were making some good time down the mountain. Kind of jumping down the mountain. The boy, the sick one, was hollering something, and I think he was puking while he was hollering, but I couldn't make it out and by the time I got over here from where we are camped at here, it was over."

Slowly, the voice connects to a woman in a camouflage sweat suit emerging from the gloom. "This is twice I've come to this site now. I always come here after the Charlotte races. Two-different-worlds-I-live-in thing. I hope you can catch up with them. Go that way and you might can get up with them before they hit the bottom."

I yell thanks as I start down the short cut. I run and brake down the path, both hands in front of me as if I had someone there to catch me, to keep me from falling. No nice cut-in steps on this one, no wide paved parts or even gravel, just roots and dirt.

As I pop out of the woods, I can see the parking lot below me. There's a blur of Rich's van tearing away.

I can't die now. Seriously. Later. Andrew's words again. I have to get in my car and follow them. I move, it seems, in slow motion through mud and snowdrifts toward my car. I have run full blast down the trail, the one I could hardly get up forty-five minutes ago.

I jump into the car. Then the ranger comes over from his station and yells in my window, "Lynchburg General, second exit." I rip the car into gear.

I am on automatic pilot. I don't see the road or the signs. The car is on a string that follows the *H* signs.

I don't want to be the crazy woman I am, I want to get out of my body, away from Lynchburg, Virginia, away from earth.

When Rich stayed out all night I would crawl, figuratively speaking, into a concrete pipe. The pipe, like the one road crews use for culverts, was very helpful to me at the time. I haven't used the pipe since I left Rich, and I don't know if it will work while I am driving. I let the pipe slip its cool heavy concrete over my shoulder. I feel its calm heaviness, the reassurance of being safe and sealed, underground. There are slits for me to see through. My legs weigh two tons each, my body sinks through the car seat, my head is dragging the highway, making sparks. I'm in my concrete pipe.

The pipe was the way I got over Rich's sex appeal: the concrete crushed it out of me. I thought it crushed all my sex appeal. I hoped so. Maybe some man from outer space would find me and we could have a date, but no earth man, no one raised in America.

The pipe got me over being married, too. If I'll ever get over it. That was harder to crush out of my head than sex. My car, like a toy car programmed to seek a certain point, drives to the hospital to find my kidnapped, dying child and his brother. But me, I'm in my nice gray concrete pipe again. I want a successful single parent's life, forget sex and marriage, just breathing children, nothing else matters. Dr. Grace Towle is my role model.

I would like to die before my kids beat me to it. A nice single parent's funeral with nice sad grown-up children with jobs they got off from to come to their mother's service. In my concrete pipe on the dark highway in the mountains, my life looks possible.

I get to the hospital and walk toward the emergency entrance. I look for my insurance card like a normal person. My professional life with old people is a help—I can read insurance cards, their group numbers, their plan codes, in the dark. I know insurance cards are more important than anything else in the world, almost anything.

I walk in the emergency entrance. I flash the card to the girl at the desk, who flips through the yellow slips on the clipboard, then punches the computer and reads from the screen, not turning to look at me.

"He's being prepped now."

"For what?"

"For the O.R. Emergency appendectomy. It burst. That's why we went ahead and started prepping without the insurance numbers. We've lost some with bursts. His father said you had the card and would be here as soon as you could, so we went ahead, against regs, but he was so insistent that you would be here immediately. And he was right, you're here. I need to punch in the numbers and photocopy your card before you go to the prep room."

Andrew is asleep, with an IV dripping in his arm. He looks younger than eight—about four, in his face—and as if he had been dipped in liquid Saran Wrap, shocked.

Has he known terrible pain before this? No broken arms, no cracked teeth from skateboarding, no burns. Just falling from the chairs when he walked from one to another, waiting for Rich to catch him.

He is in a space just big enough for the bed, with curtains hanging on a metal pipe around him, hardly enough room for me to stand inside the curtain. I look under the sheet at his stomach to see if I can see anything wrong. Smooth and perfect.

Three other cubicles of space are curtained off in the big room.

No Richie. No Rich. But at least, for the moment, I know where Andrew is.

While I was hurtling down the mountain and to the hospital, I knew Andrew and Richie were just ahead, and if I could go faster, I'd catch them. It is a funny kind of happiness to find one of them alive. I know that Richie is alive too, and somewhere near me.

Mama's sister, Aunt Marie, the one who called out the troop of alcoholics to find Daddy the time he got lost, always used to say that things would certainly get worse, that was the one thing we knew for sure. She used to stare out the window and would add, "Enjoy what you have." Now, with half my children in front of me, alive, fifty percent of my child population, I am happier, much, than I had been.

One of Andrew's journal entries comes to mind. I tore it out and carry it in my wallet. I have memorized it. I can see my influence on him, my good influence, looking for small happinesses in life:

My Life Today
Today is a very good because I have to leave school erly because of my brothers basketball game. I think we will get to see him play. Luckily my mom got seson tickets to all the games. Another good thing is that I have no homework over the weekend. And that's my life today.

The nurse—Beth, according to her name tag—opens the curtain. "We need you to step out to the waiting room so we can take Andrew down to surgery and fix him up. As soon as Dr. Rogers scrubs, we'll be set. You will be given some literature on ruptured appendices so you will understand the risks involved; then you will have to sign the release. In this case, because of the perforation, it would be better to sign the release first, and then read the literature. His father has signed one, but in divorce situations, we've found that it's a good idea to have both parents, if available, sign. From the perspective of legalities, it's for the best. Has your son had a history of pain in the abdominal area?"

Beth smiles at me as if we were at a high school reunion. I can tell she is a jogger and aerobics person, a junior Dr. Towle. Then she adds, "Don't worry, children are Jesus' first concern. He suffered them to come unto him. Jesus is watching over your Andrew and has him in his hand."

She slips back out, holding the curtain back the way they do on the *Tonight* show for the guests, so I slip out with her. I want to answer the question about Andrew's history of pain, but she is hurrying away.

"How long will the operation take," I ask her uniformed back.

Turning, she says, "No time, about an hour, if there are no complications. We want to be careful because of the rupture, the spread of infection, and we must hurry. Please sign the papers I left at the desk."

At the big curved bar of a desk papers are clipped on a board with a happy-face stick-on that reads, "For the Mom to sign." There is an X at the line for my signature. Rich has signed his name on the line above. I have no idea where I am in the hospital.

There is an underground tunnel, like my concrete pipe, to the coffee shop, all decorated for Halloween, though someone has begun to take the twisted black and orange streamers down and to put up Thanksgiving Puritans and turkeys.

People are ordering breakfast. Maybe they have dead children and don't know what else to do.

It is seven minutes to ten, on the big clock. Some people are eating lasagna—one of Andrew's spelling words last week when they were doing food words: wonton, tortilla, spaghetti, mousse, soufflé, chow mein. Weren't they hard words for third-graders? He said Ms. Sowers was giving him special help because he had told her I said he needed it. "I don't think you need 'special' help and don't use that word," I yelled.

Why did I yell about spelling words, to a child who was smart enough to ask for help, who only wanted a little extra attention?

I get a tray full of breakfast food. Hospitals have people who are starting the day around-the-clock. Orange juice, scrambled eggs, bacon and sausage cakes, whole wheat toast. The food makes me feel normal just to look at it. I pretend it's early morning, I am just starting out for a normal day. I will eat, or look at, anyway, an all-American breakfast.

Rich. I decide not to think about him for a minute, just the fifty percent of my children I know is safe. The gulp of the juice scalds my throat.

I will put off dying, eat a forkful of scrambled egg. During Andrew's operation, I will clean my plate. I will think things through. I will think straight. I will keep my promise, the one I shrieked on the Peaks of Otter. The one about not moving again. Maybe not the one about forgiving everybody.

How did Rich know I would get to the hospital with the insurance card? How did he know I would be able to make it across the state, find the campground, the hospital in Lynchburg?

That's easy, I say to myself, blowing my coffee. Rich thinks that as their mother, I somehow know what is necessary to know, not what I may want to know, but life-or-death necessary stuff. A parent, in his book, is magic. He or she, especially he, can tell what children need. Like a trip to the Peaks of Otter. Remember, he helped Andrew call me. He doesn't think I will know things through the air, ESP, exactly. But he knew after the call I would put two and two together and get up here. He could probably tell by the time Andrew called that something was wrong, that he might need me to get up here quickly. He hadn't figured, I'm sure, on the emergency, just the flu or something that might make it hard to go on having fun—his main idea when it comes to kids.

The hospital is an unexpected detail, one I had to figure out. And if Rich had had time, he would have called me himself. I bet he did, but by then I had left for the mountains.

I ask myself as I bite the crust of toast with the last piece of bacon wrapped up in it if Rich will show up while the operation is going on. Will he wait with me? Will he tell me where Richie is? Will Richie be with him?

The answer comes to me like a voice from across the table, a kind but invisible friend. "He'll send Richie in to wait with you. Now they're out eating a steak or shrimp. He's building Richie's strength up for a long night of waiting with a hysterical mother. No, Rich himself won't come. He knows it'd make you worse. But he'll keep watching, and he'll visit Andrew when you're out of the room, here in the underground cafeteria eating with all these grieving people." The friendly voice sounds like the radio voice of the star man, a little like Douglas Smathers's voice.

I ask my ghost companion silently if we could get a police guard for Andrew's room.

The answer floats across the table on the coffee vapor. No. It would take the judge, a lawyer. It'd take a few days, and Andrew will be home by then. It's better to let Rich go for now, and just get Andrew through this. Don't scatter your attention thinking about Rich. You're too tired to fuss at Richie even. This kind of life is turning your children into liars, not in words, maybe, but in situations. They knew all during the school program last night that they were leaving; they'd already packed. Ruth, you look a hundred years old.

I am a hundred years old. I thought I could wear Rich down, by moving, but I am sure now that I cannot keep on moving. Rich cannot give up the boys, as other fathers do across America.

I go on telling myself what I already know, but it helps to sit there in the hospital, thinking in conversations with myself, helpless to do anything but sit.

It is not me, really, that Rich has been chasing, it is his idea of our little family. I know the way his brain works. His whole family was like that. Who do you think is paying for the shrimp or steak dinner tonight? His mother. She wants him to have his boys. I think she must have hated me for ruining the McFall idea of family. I wasn't Phyllis Joyner, but I would do, would have to, and I have the two grandsons, the precious blood descendents.

I return to the present for a minute and ask myself about any troubles Andrew has been having. Sure, Andrew had missed a few days of school, but it was so he could get to do makeup work and get extra help from the teacher, carry notes back and forth, and get a conference set up for us all to sit down and discuss his work and his adjustment to school. When he would say his stomach hurt, I thought he just needed, as Ms. Sowers herself said, some extra attention, so I'd let him go to work with me and watch TV with the residents or help me put up a new bulletin board. The pains went away by lunchtime, usually. I took him to the doctor once—not to Grace; I didn't know her then—but he just smiled and said he thought Andrew was having a tough time in the third grade, a diagnosis Andrew loved because it meant more notes and conferences. It was clear that doctor thought he was a little hypochondriac. I do not feel Grace would have dismissed Andrew's description of the pain. He called it a "warm bubble." She would have asked him questions and called for more tests, I bet.

The pains were real. It was chronic appendicitis.

My lips move like Andrew's when he reads. I think I have a learning disability.

From the corner of the cafeteria, high on the wall, comes the voice that calls doctors and nurses away from their meals and coffee breaks, only it's calling for me. I think of the old hymn, "Softly and sweetly, Jesus is calling, calling for you and for me." I hope Jesus is not calling Andrew home, because if he is, he is going to have to call me too. Richie will have to live here on earth alone, with his father.

When I get to the phone, the operator asks if I am me.

"Yes, I am." I want to add, "But not for long. It depends."

She says I should come to Room 418 immediately.

IX

*A*ndrew looks dead. His chest isn't moving. Maybe he has died when no one was looking. He is stretched flat on the bed and tucked in tightly under his arms, which lie on top of the sheets straight down, like spare parts to another body.

An IV stand with a rack for two plastic bags filled with clear liquid guards his bed. Tubes run to a taped place at the vein in the crook of his left arm.

He is packaged, ready to be shipped away. I touch the tip of his right shoulder. Warm. His head is cocked down on his chest, and I move it a little so his neck doesn't look broken. I kiss the stubble of his Mohawk.

Dead baby jokes—Andrew's favorites—come back to me: How do you make a dead baby float? One glass of Coke and one scoop of dead baby.

Andrew doesn't trust me. "You always forget. Remember the time you were going to pick me up after school to go to the mall. I had invited two new friends to go, but you didn't show up and then the teacher came out to the front of the school and said you weren't coming? You said you would pick me up. With my friends." His eyes can kick up a storm when he gets going, but they are shut now.

No wonder his dad looks so good, always showing up. Unlike his mom, he is someone who invariably shows up, like magic, on a roof, at a window, bringing dogs, thinking up a camping trip.

"He's here, he hasn't slipped away. He's okay." The nurse is smiling.

A hot shower has been turned on in my brain. Pure happiness, spraying down through my neck to my arms and legs.

She hands me a sheaf of brochures to read about kids and surgery, appropriate gifts for the hospital, sleep-in moms, and, near the end of each brochure, the dangers of any surgery. How it can kill anyone under certain conditions.

Beth, the nurse, comes in to say it will be about two hours before Andrew wakes up, and then he will be groggy and disoriented, so if I want to go anywhere, I should go now. She assures me that he has done fine in surgery. Dr. Rogers will tell me more.

"Where would I go at almost midnight?"

"My church has open sanctuary. People come to talk to the Lord day and night. You probably have many things on your heart to share with Him at this point. There's a mall, too, if you need to shop. It's open until two."

Beth smiles her reunion smile. I am feeling so good, I almost say yes, I'll go to her church. Beth probably has helped save Andrew's life. I am sure she has. She looks as if she could save anyone.

"I'll just sit here a while, I think. Thank you for telling me about your church and the mall." I sound sickeningly sweet, but I like it. Beth must have too.

"Okay, little mom. You stay by your big baby. All we have to do is fight off that old infection, which the literature will explain, and then he'll be back on his feet. Three weeks is usual for the perforated cases. See you in a little. Andrew is mine until morning, so I'll check in on you every ten minutes or so."

Isn't she wonderful? I ask myself, this nurse, who is someone I would normally hate or envy. I remember that I have a friend, Grace, who has this same medical confidence. Maybe I have something to offer medical professionals. I mean, maybe they see something in me that needs fixing, needs help. I wonder for a second if Douglas Smathers has ever studied medicine. I make a note deep in my brain to ask him. Here at Andrew's hospital bed, I love Beth and her Jesus and her all-night-open sanctuary very much. I ESP some love to Grace Towle, too.

There is a heavy fold-out chair by the bed. It takes Beth two heaves and a violent jerk to put it down into a cot with big gaps in it. She tells me to go to sleep, and I do what she says. I am hypnotized by her smiles.

In two hours, I have slept a century when Andrew starts waking up. He has a worried look on his face. His lips move and he groans. I have read about children living secret lives that would shock their parents. Usually the surprise is drugs and drinking. I can believe it, but I don't think Andrew is drinking or taking crack yet.

"Mom," he says, which kills me. I am used to getting all of Andrew's love from his eyes while I listen to his complaints.

I look at his hands. They are dirty but okay as far as I can see. They can bend. "Mom," he says again. The word sounds newly oiled. I have never heard him say that word without the rust of disappointment covering it.

While I am bending Andrew's fingers, Richie walks in and stands at the foot of the bed, looking six feet tall.

"Where have you been?" The force of my question is lost among the curtained beds and IVs.

"With Dad. You know that, Mom. He took us camping. We were only going for the weekend. We called you. You knew about it, kind of, and then we called. We just wanted to go and Dad thought it'd be okay. If we'd asked, you would have said no. You know you would. You always say no. We had good camping stuff, and it wasn't far from you. Just a few hours. Look how quick you found us. But then Andrew got really sick, and so fast, it scared me. It scared Dad, too. We've been asleep, well, not really asleep, in his van parked next to the hospital in case Andrew needed us. Are you okay? It's three-thirty in the morning."

I struggle to get closer to Richie, but I keep bashing my ankles on the cold metal frame of the cot.

Richie seems elongated, reflected in a crazy-house mirror, all long bones and deep eyes. He is about to cry. Unlike Andrew, Richie never blames me for anything. He feels sorry for me. He looks ancient. He doesn't blame me for the divorce; he is sorry I felt I had to get one.

I hold his hand across the corner of Andrew's bed. He reaches for me and pats me, as he always does, but this time I don't say my usual don't-pat-me-I'm-not-a-dog.

"I'm getting us another dog. We'll have three dogs. What do you think of that? Will you run off camping or skydiving if I get another dog? You know Douglas P. Smathers, your friend? We had a date. He's taking care of the dogs we already have."

"No, Mom, go slow. We don't need another dog. We've already got three dogs—with Dad's. You don't have to go on dates. Don't go overboard on us. Don't overload the circuits."

"The dogs can watch you and Andrew play Nintendo. Maybe they can help me with the cooking. I'll teach them to broil chicken."

Richie smiles, not sure whether I am joking or have finally lost it.

"I can't go on having sad children who have to arrange for their own kidnapping in order to have some fun, can I? I can't go on being tricked into getting dogs, having your father visit on the roof. Don't you think enough is enough?"

There is nothing else to say, nothing I know how to say, nothing Richie can do anything about.

He can't help being who he is, the terrible combination of me and his father. He looks, even as sad and sorry as he is, like Rich's and my best selves, when we were the beautiful children of a million years back, swinging through dry creek beds in August, building lean-tos against the peeling sycamore trees that stretched out over the Tar River. We were going to build a cabin there later, then a wharf for the fleet of canoes and rafts that would tie up for the night. Our playing was serious. It got the sex started, which got our lives started toward this hospital room with one dead-looking boy in the bed, and an old-looking boy at its foot.

Seeing Richie, dirty and haggard, and seeing all he means without knowing any of it, in the planes of his face, in the set of his shoulders, snaps my heart in two like a dry stick. I know he will never leave again without telling me. I know I am not moving again, moving just to stay ahead of Rich. Our childhood sweethearthood is over, dead.

Dr. Rogers says that Andrew can be moved to Richmond so we can go on with our lives. He should be in a hospital for close to a week in case his temperature spikes.

"Get Richie back in school. Get Andrew's homework so he can do his work in bed."

He keeps rubbing Andrew's head backwards, the way I love to because of the soft Mohawk bristles, and talking the educated redneck way that the doctors talk who come to Elder Home.

"Come on, good buddy, you done real good. You'll be looking good in no time and back on the road again. You're a lucky son, real good and lucky. If you'd been ten minutes later getting to me, we'd be in deep water in a leaky boat."

Nurse Beth returns. Her favorite word is "little."

"And here are a few little things for you, Little Mom, a few little items for moms that we keep on hand for just such occasions as these."

Dr. Rogers and Nurse Beth seem to know a lot about us. We all smile. I can tell Richie feels better, so I take the care kit. I need it. My teeth are furry, and I look like a reduced-for-quick-sale item at the grocery store.

"Mom, go take a quick little shower down the hall. I'll watch our boy." Beth smiles.

After the shower, even in my dirty, wrinkled clothes, I feel better, a little better, eighty instead of a hundred years old. When I get back to Andrew's room, Richie is gone. My knees buckle.

Beth answers without my asking her. "He's gone with his father back to the camp to gather up the gear. His father came in to check on him before you got here. They'll be back in a little while. They said for you not to worry."

Beth helps me get the cot folded back up into a chair and I sit down and try not to worry. I imagine the three of us, with Dr. Rogers and Beth along for a crew, in a concrete pipe. We are in an underground shelter, fully equipped for life in one place for a long time: food, television, Nintendo machine, three dogs, dog food, frozen chicken. Rich will come visit every Tuesday evening and sit in the parlor section of the pipe. Like Rachel, I will have parties. We will fox-trot up and down the pipe. At ten, Rich will leave, thanking me for the nice visit. We will surface like a submarine every morning so that I can go to work. The boys will go to school, go to soccer, and return to their nice sunken concrete pipe, carpeted, cushioned, portholed.

The Wrench will recover from his asthma and bring his mother over for a visit, when they will be delighted to have pizza with Ms. Vincent and Ms. Sowers. Douglas P. Smathers and Officer Armentrout will also be there. Alonzo Johnson will be there without a splint on his fingers. Subterranean flowers will bloom.

Holding Andrew's wrist with my fingers on his pulse, I think about our nomadic lives, all two states' worth—from Tarboro to Rocky Mount to Roxbury to South Boston, to Clarksville, to Danville to Richmond. Other towns.

"Mom," Andrew is mumbling. His lips are dry and puffy. I can rub a gelatin stick on them, Beth said, but not a drop of water.

"Here I am. It's your appendix, old man, old stump knocker, old pulpwood truck." I am talking redneck myself, like Dr. Rogers. I rub the pink sponge with gelatin on it across Andrew's lips. He smiles a little. I go on calling him names, "Ocean eyes, chain saw, twenty-two rifle, five-point buck, four in the floor and a fifth under the seat." He smiles again but doesn't open his eyes.

"Mom."

We both go back to sleep, and it seems two days later when we wake up again. Andrew is sick, and mad that he hurts so bad. I can tell he thinks I had something to do with the pain. I feel as if I were floating around outside my body. Outside the concrete pipe. Light and watery in my bones.

"I'll go see if you can have a drink now." His lips are cracked open, his skin has a dry sheen to it. Beth is not around the desk. She has gone off duty at seven.

"A few sips, and I mean sips," says the new nurse, Ms. Tawarna Brown, R.N. "Not water either." Tawarna does not move her lips or her body when she speaks. "There's Coke in the refrigerator in the kitchen across from his room. A few, two maybe, sips."

Andrew can hardly stand the sips of Coke. When I lift his head up, tears pop out of his eyes. He points to his stomach, the thick bandage.

"Am I pulling your muscle, old man?"

Ocean Eyes, all bright with tears, looks yes at me.

I stick the tip of the gelatin sponge into the Coke and wipe it across his lips. It stings. Andrew jerks in slow motion to save his cut muscles—still, it tastes good to him.

"You had your appendix taken out, and now it's all over. You'll need extra help from your teachers, I bet."

Andrew looks at me with what would be called tolerance if he were older. He shakes his head slightly and puts his tongue on his bottom lip. I dab some more Coke on it.

Andrew looks at me and whispers, "Where's Richie?"

"He's gone with your father back to the mountain to get the tent and camping stuff, which reminds me of how you deliberately deceived me, your own mama, just like the kids I read about in the newspaper who sell drugs and get shot by pushers."

"Shut up, Mom." He smiles and closes his eyes but asks me if the other kids in his room have had the same operation. I say I don't know, but I'll find out.

I go to each bed and knock little dents in the curtains that hang around them. Each has a child and a mother standing by a fold-up cot. One skinny kid has his mother and grandmother with him. They look to have been there a while, because the room resembles a wrecked toy shop. Balloons and stuffed animals are tied to IV poles and curtain rods.

Lamont sends out for pizza and fries because he can't stand the hospital food. He is giving his big sister some of his bone marrow, he says. She is upstairs on the cancer floor, and when he goes up there, he gets to wear a suit and mask. His mom and "Big Mom" bring all his meals in from fast-food places.

Andrew looks impressed with Lamont's coolness. Across from us is Jarrod. His head looks soft and squashed, as if it had an invisible rubber band around it. He is eleven but weighs only forty-five pounds. His mother is beautiful and sleeps in the bed with him instead of in the cot. He speaks in little snorts that she interprets. When his father comes to visit, the three of them lie on the hospital bed, watching the hanging television, laughing at Cosby. Jarrod's father has brought five hundred dollars from his slow-pitch ball club, and they spread the bills out on the bed, smoothing them out and putting the tens with the tens, the fives with the fives, and so on, as if they were playing Monopoly.

Marcellus is catercornered from us. His appendix has burst too. He is fourteen and cries a crooning dry-eyed cry most of the time. Like

Lamont, he sends out for food. His mother is pregnant, won't be thirty until next June, she says, has a comb stuck upside down in her hair. She talks mean to Marcellus, who croons back to her, "You don't mean it, Mumma, you don't mean it." Every now and then she stomps out in a storm of cursing, yelling what she is going to do to him when she gets him home. When she sees me listening, she stops and says slowly to him, "Can I help you, Baby?" When she sees I am not judging her, she tells me it gets old real fast to stay in the hospital and she's been there two and a half weeks. She has a two-year-old at home and is expecting, so she doesn't need the hospital and Marcellus carrying on like he is crazy.

With the curtains all swung open, we are a sight. I can see how I look to the black women: I am a woman who has no idea what to do with a child. Even Marcellus's mother looks at me with pity. Jarrod's mother, who sits cross-legged in the bed and irons her shirts on a pillow in her lap so she'll look nice and fresh for Jarrod, and for his father when he drives in from Martinsville—four and a half hours away—looks at me with a kind of pity.

I can translate their looks into something like "Look, you've got that nice, big boy. Now do something for him. Go buy him some real food, some balloons."

I feel like answering them back. "I haven't had time to fill up his curtain rod with hanging stuffed dogs and dinosaurs. I swear I will send out for supper for Andrew as soon as he can eat."

I give him another sponge dip of Coke. I say, as much for the other mothers' benefit as for Andrew's, "I'm getting you a Nintendo."

"Mom, how are the puppies. Tell Dad and Richie to go home and take care of them, okay?"

Andrew drifts away. He doesn't look as dead now. I can't answer him anyway. He does not know that Douglas Smathers is taking care of the dogs.

Andrew's eyes open again. "The puppies would have been happy, I bet, happier than even us, running up and down mountains, fighting with trees. I told Richie to bring them along. We were, all of us, having a good time, Mom." Andrew's voice is woozy and slow.

"The puppies would love, you're right, being in the mountains and on a trip with you, but Elder would get carsick, I bet," I answer him slowly. "Douglas Smathers, your friend, and now my friend, is looking after the dogs. Don't worry. They will be fine."

I look up and see the mothers and sick children looking at us. They are very interested. I pull the curtain around us.

"Andrew, you and Richie went off and left me without telling me a word. I almost went crazy."

"I know. But didn't you find our note?"

Andrew is drifting off again, leaving me with a note to find. A note changes everything. If they really did write me a note, then they are not the pre-criminals I think they are bound to be, genetically. The note means responsibility has taken root in their souls. The note changes my whole life. I realize I have not seen this note, that it was not in any obvious place in the apartment. Douglas Smathers did not find any note. We always leave messages stuck under magnets on the refrigerator, and I remember staring at it when we got back the second time from the school. But if there is a piece of paper in the apartment that has gotten itself under a sweatshirt or a shoe, then my sons are not ricocheting through their childhood, wild and headed for a terrible life. They did not leave me without a word.

Listening to myself, I can hear what a family counselor would say about how it is necessary to believe the best, to take little leaps of faith. Whenever it was at all possible, a mother, especially a single one, should at the very least not think the worst, as I usually do. No note means Andrew and Richie are clones of Rich, ready to leave me, thinking their father is a better parent than I am, thinking I will get over their going away, thinking they can go and come whenever Rich pulls up in his van. No note means they want me out of the picture. Get Mom a date, for instance. Get some puppies for her to take care of. With a note, all this changes: They went camping—simply met their father and took a short trip to the mountains.

I am an expert on the way counselors hear things, and how they talk. I learned from going to sessions by myself. Rich said, "Be my guest, go on, I'm staying married." He said the minute you started going to marriage counselors you better call your attorney, so I went by myself for the six years we were married, off and on, and he was wrong—I didn't get a lawyer until after I left.

The thought of the boys writing me a note about where they were going, how long they would be away, loosens my brain from my skull. The note frees me to think. It is clear now, in the hospital, that I must have gotten used to Rich's presence. I must have liked it in some horrible way, needed it, in fact. Divorce, for me, was a new way of being married. Bingo! I see it all. So it took a kidnapping and surgery to get my deepest attention. So I have a learning disability. At least I am finally getting the picture.

One of the last marriage counselors told me that married people did not know themselves, that they were strangers to themselves, simply because, as I understood it, they were in a marriage, which was like being in a foreign country. "Would you be the same person in Afghanistan that you are here?" this counselor asked me. Then, before I could answer, she nodded to herself. "The same is true of the person in a marriage." This counselor had a thing about Afghanistan, because no matter what I said, she would shake her head and ask me about living in Kabul. She always spoke of the state of marriage as a place, especially Kabul, where you learned a certain language, customs, rituals, guerrilla warfare, sabotage, a different way of dressing. I lasted only two sessions with her, but Afghanistan stuck with me.

Why aren't there divorce counselors? I have been to counselors at groups called Family Practices, a name that always makes me think of voodoo or something with animal sacrifices. I need a group called Divorce Practices.

In retrospect, I think that talking to lawyers and cops is more helpful than talking with marriage counselors. Cops don't care why you shot someone; they just tell you what to do next. Like Officer Armentrout calling me and telling me to come to Laburnum Avenue because there had been a bike accident or stopping me to tell me to replace my license sticker. The counselors I knew always wanted to help me "work through" things, come to my own conclusions.

In the time by Andrew's bed, picturing the precious note he'd mentioned and thinking about all those sessions of tears in counselors' offices, I feel my fears lift off my heart. Andrew and Richie had left me a note telling me everything. We have a good life is what it really said, I'm sure, between the lines telling me the facts, where and when.

Praise Jesus, I want to yell to Nurse Beth. My boys were not running away from me! They were not kidnapped. Just camping for the weekend. Happy, happy American children, a little careless about Mom, but happy, happy boys. Huck Finning through their lives. A note to Mom makes everything okay. They are right.

My children are not runaways. They did not deceive their hard-working mother, who needs to trust them more than she needs anything else.

I have been so sure that I had already let go of being married to Rich a long time ago. With each move, I thought I was letting go of another piece of our marriage, throwing overboard another suitcase.

Wrong again, drink some gin, begin again, as the boys chorus in rap.

At last, I am leaving the foreign country of marriage, I am an Afghan refugee, I am heading back to America, which is to say, Divorce Country—it all hits me, like a beanbag at one of Rachel's parties. Between the eyes, hard, so it hurts. Rachel handed out bean-bags to us at her winter parties. And once, Rich and James and the Marshall and Blair cousins went wild, ran outside and nearly killed each other, throwing them like baseballs. They came back into the house with deep scratches on their cheeks and necks, all hot and red, sweating in the cold house. Then we fox-trotted, hot and cold, and blood got on our faces from the boys, and Rachel had a better time than usual. I think she loved for things to get a little out of hand, go almost crazy. Phyllis would never go to Rachel's parties, and they were the only public or social places, not counting school, where I saw Rich.

I feel as if I were hanging from the rope in my dream and being hit by the beanbags as I stand by Andrew's bed, my brain going crazy over a note I hope and pray exists.

I open the green curtains. I feel like a refugee setting foot on the shores of America, divorced, bruised, and alone, but ready for what-ever happens next. I come in for a landing from the rope Rich pulled me up on. I float down by myself, without Rachel.

I smile at the mothers and children in the beds around the room, and they smile back, waiting, I guess, for Act Two to begin. Dr. Grace Towle must often have a feeling close to this—people in beds, waiting for a word or gesture, for medicine, for hope.

It isn't long before Nurse Beth makes her entrance and Ms.

Tawarna Brown goes off duty, pulling behind her a fleet of balloons and a bag of presents.

"Don't wake him up." She hugs me, dropping all her stuff and tying the balloons to the IV pole. The mothers look on approvingly. I know the balloons are from Rich, but what can I say?

If only I were dressed for the part of a good mother, in an apricot silk shirt, harem pants, and short boots, had big leather tote bags and an oversize suede jacket, the color of caramel. If only I looked like a rock star, I think they would approve of me more.

My big hair is hitting the IV pole, so I tie it down under the big red handkerchief Douglas stuffed into my hip pocket as I left. "Reflex action," he said, and muttered something about how his family always gave people a little something just as they left, no matter how small, no matter how unhelpful. Would I take his bandanna handkerchief? Sure, why not?

Andrew looks dead again and scares me into thinking straight, about the present, not the past of Rachel's parties, the rope, even Douglas Smathers's family good-byes. I stop thinking about what I should look like and start seeing in black and white that we are in a hospital ninety-three miles from home. I concentrate on my new insurance benefits with the emergency room deductible of a hundred dollars.

At home, I swear to myself, we will stop all the secrets, stop the undercover life my boys have been living—have been forced to live in order to see their crazy father, who maybe just acts crazy because I keep moving. Maybe I really can stop moving like a crazy woman, like some migrant worker. Maybe I can have teachers over for supper on a regular basis. Maybe Dr. Towle will come and tell me why she adopted The Wrench. Maybe Douglas Smathers will come over for a regular date, not an overnighter when he has to cook breakfast and stuff a red handkerchief in my jeans as I set off on a journey to find my lost kids, like someone in a modern Grimm's fairy tale, a poor peasant mother whose sons, lost in the forest, are really the lost princes.

Maybe we can calm down and act normal, have routines.

Maybe I will give Rich a key to the apartment so he can help take care of the dogs. Am I going too far?

By this time, I am talking out loud to myself. I pull the heavy green curtain. "Show's over, folks. More at eleven."

X

*B*y the first of December, Andrew will be back in school, having missed exactly one month. He will be happy with all the adjustment problems he has to face with the help of Ms. Sowers: no gym class, extra assignments to make up his work, especially a papier-mâché model of Plymouth Rock. Elder and Home will carry the rock from room to room, eating its edges as if it were a big piece of candy.

During November, while he is at home recuperating, a visiting teacher, Ms. Woods, comes and sits by the bed to let Andrew dictate his reports. She says dictation is a good learning method and builds confidence, and Andrew does look like a rich kid with a secretary, propped up on pillows, his black dogs sleeping on either side of him. He asks Ms. Woods if she has gotten down all of his last sentence, and she reads it back to him, checking to see if she has gotten his every syllable. She brings him messages from Ms. Sowers, and Andrew receives them as if they were debriefings from a diplomatic pouch.

He entertains from his bed, and The Wrench joins him for peer tutoring sessions, which Ms. Sowers and Ms. Woods both have recommended. When The Wrench has an asthma attack and misses school, he and Andrew stay on the phone, their bedside phones. Once when I answer the phone by mistake—all calls are for Andrew—I ask The Wrench how he keeps up with his assignments since he misses so much school. He laughs a wise, kindly laugh and explains to me that he is lucky to have a photographic memory and an IQ of just under genius level, 147. I say I thought IQ testing had gone out with the ark, and he says I'm right, it had, but still it is useful to a student to know exactly what, even if a poor measuring instrument is used, he can expect of himself. The Wrench, he says, expects straight A's, and with grades, expectation is half the battle. Knowing his test results, he says, helps him. His mother gives him an IQ test whenever he feels the need for a shot of energy. Seeing that number, even if it means very little, is like—here The Wrench pauses—reading a horoscope or playing the Ouija board. Do I know what he means? I guess I do, I tell him.

He comes to visit, to spend the night, sick or well. "It doesn't matter. I have to breathe no matter where I am. It's simply a breathing disorder, not contagious, and I would love to come, if it's all right with you, Mrs. McFall." He and Andrew like to read their collections of get-well cards, play the Nintendo set up in his room, look at the scar from the operation, and feel the invisible hair ridge of bike-accident-broken collarbone. I can never feel the broken bone.

"Can't I get you boys some baseball cards? Wouldn't they be more fun than get-well cards, more like the rest of the boys in America?" I try to be funny. They look at me, distracted by my interruption of their friendship, sitting like skinny Buddhas in the bed, a dog apiece, studying their collections.

"Mom, we are different. Can't you see that?"

They like to use The Wrench's portable breathing machine, which he brings along with new Nintendo games and a change of clothes. I hear them tell each other, over and over, their tales of pain and suffering.

"You two will make good old people, great ones, the way you know your aches and pains." I try to joke with them.

"We will be old together," The Wrench says. "We've planned it all out. We're lucky and we have this sick thing in common, which is very fortunate. We do not mind being sick or, we guess, getting old. Do we, Andrew?"

"No, we like being sick. We will like being old."

"I don't think it's healthy for children to like being sick or look forward to old age. Come to Elder Home with me when you are well, and I will show you some things about old age that will scare you. I bet Dr. Towle has no idea that her son *likes* being sick. It's weird, if you ask me, to like being in bed."

"You don't understand, Mom. We don't like the sick part or the bed part, but we like making the best of it. Finding stuff to do we didn't know we could do."

"Like what?"

"I forget, but lots of stuff. When I think of something, I'll let you know what."

I say thanks and then they go on with their accounts of their awful experiences. "It felt like a frozen knife that would get real, real hot, burning hot; then I would puke, which made it worse, much worse." The Wrench presses on his stomach to see if he is lucky enough to have discovered an early sign of appendicitis.

Richie approves of the flair for drama his brother is developing. Maybe he can be in the next Parents Be Pushers Back program. Douglas drops by to enjoy the scenes from family life. Now and then, Grace shows up to retrieve The Wrench, but most of the time I drop him off when he has to go home. I've always heard women say that after two children, you don't notice more, and it's true. In fact, The Wrench makes it easier, breaks the tension between the blood brothers. Sometimes Grace calls to say she will be late and apologizes for asking if he can spend another night with us.

"He loves being over at your place. Sometimes, I think he wants you to adopt him, or maybe adopt him *and* me so we could all live together. I'm not around a whole lot, as you know, so I wouldn't be much trouble."

I take this opportunity to ask Grace how she came to be the mother of our new best friend.

"It's too long to tell you over the phone, which is where I spend some of the most relaxing times of my life these days," she sighs, "talking to you, I mean. Come to lunch this weekend and I will try to explain what The Wrench and I often wonder about—how we got together. It's a miracle or, as he says, superweird."

I have never been called "relaxing" in my life. It is a Rocky Mountain high. Am I someone I do not know? To other people, is it possible that I have qualities I never suspected I possessed?

I look in on the two invalids sleeping with two dogs. They are both superweirdos, but lying there with the dogs' noses pointed straight toward the foot of the bed, they are beautiful. The Wrench's hair, black like his adopted mother's, against the pillow, Andrew's growing-out Mohawk, their faces with their brains turned off are beautiful. Flowerlike. They would hate to hear my thoughts.

I visit Grace in her condo one Saturday while Andrew and The Wrench rest and drink fluids with the dogs at my apartment. Her condo is all whites and grays and efficiency, designed to make whoever comes in feel sci-fi modern and more intelligent than usual. I want to ask for an IQ test myself after I have been there twenty minutes.

I hear the story of how she got The Wrench. It's a story that will give me something to think about for years, when I am an old lady in an Elder Home, should I make it that long. It will take me that long to believe it. It seems that Grace had a best friend in college, a Wrenn Chauncey, who could never settle down, lived her life to a different drumbeat, got herself "impregnated," Grace called it, by a student who wanted to marry her, but she laughed at him. No, Wrenn wanted a baby, had the baby, and then fell apart when she met the baby. Perfect Lamaze delivery, forty-five-minute labor, friends around, the father there weeping and begging her to marry him, unbelievable. Champagne in the delivery room—that's a new one on me. But it didn't work. A baby is a frightening thing to see, and I guess Wrenn Chauncey could see what she was looking at.

Grace says quietly that it happens—rejection of the infant—and more often than I might believe.

When Wrenn got home with the baby, she went into a severe depression. Her parents set her up in the apartment she wanted, interviewed and got the perfect nannie-nurse. Money was not a problem. Classic postpartum depression. Couldn't move, couldn't look at this beautiful boy baby, called, from the moment she saw him, The Wrench, meaning monkey wrench. She couldn't speak, just cried. Dropped down to ninety-two pounds. Intervention and adoption were called for. Grace stepped forward.

As inadequate as she often feels, Grace said, The Wrench is her life. First The Wrench, then medicine.

She serves me coffee with almonds ground up in it and orange sections in a bowl Wrenn sent them from Florence, Italy, where she now works in art restoration.

I am in a daze; the caffeine has attacked my capacity to take in this information. I do not want to take an intelligence test. The doctor goes on quietly.

"The Wrench is legally mine. Spiritually or whatever, he belongs to his biological mother and to me. We write every week and spend holidays together. It's hard to believe. I don't tell many people. In fact, Ruth, you are the first person I have voluntarily told the story to. There are, of course, people who have to be told. And the asthma, of course, comes with the territory. The Wrench and I agree as to its causes. He is much better since he met you and your sons. Visiting with you, having your Andrew as a friend, and Richie, too, has helped him more than I can ever tell you. The bike accident was, he and I believe, an effort on his part to attract Andrew and Richie's attention. He says they have so much on their minds, so many things to pay attention to, that he had to "jerk them around" to get them to see him, or to get himself in their line of vision. Oh yes, he staged it, the bike wreck, down to the last detail, to attract attention. Andrew and Richie's." Her voice gets quieter and her words slower as she sees my surprise.

Then the doctor comes over to me and hugs me in a formal way. Hugging is replacing taps and pats and handshakes in our nation, but this hug is genuine. We have another almond coffee from Italy.

Mid-November brings another incredible story.

Rich sends Andrew a new telephone that looks like a race car to replace the old clunker by his bed. After one long conversation with his father, Andrew tells me Rich is getting married to a woman named Pinkie who lives in a mansion with about thirty dogs. There are stables filled with horses, an indoor soccer field, pools, a helicopter.

I don't say anything but "That's nice."

The Wrench says it sounds interesting. We all look at him. Interesting is such a mild word for him, but we let it pass. It is, in fact,

interesting that Rich is going to marry a thirty-dogged woman named
Pinkie. There isn't much else, really, to say.

The month goes up in the smoke of convalescence. The first
Thanksgiving of the new era, as I call it, is acknowledged awkwardly
by the boys' asking when it would suit me for them to be with Rich,
who has invited The Wrench to come too, and when it would suit me
for them to be at home on their four-day holiday. They have invited
The Wrench to come to our Thanksgiving. Do I want to invite his
mom, and maybe Douglas Smathers, too?

I begin to yell but catch myself. "Yes," I say in a flat, unyelling
voice, "you may visit Rich, you may even microwave a turkey in his
van on Thanksgiving Day, or visit the mansion of the rich woman he's
going to marry. Take The Wrench with you. I'll work for Mrs. Osborne at Elder Home, but you have to be here for our turkey, cooked
in the real oven, on Friday night. I have invited Douglas P. Smathers
to have dinner with us. And I will invite Dr. Towle. Douglas likes to
hear us tell stories. Grace Towle thinks I am relaxing to be around.
I have friends too, you know."

"That's cool," Richie says. He does not mention the Pinkie person,
marriage, helicopters, or anything. I think he is beginning to know his
father a little in the ways I know him.

Getting Andrew up to speed, as Dr. Rogers had called it, takes a
lot of work. I am making huge efforts to straighten out our new lives.
The time in bed gets Andrew to do better academically than he ever
has. Ms. Sowers calls and sends notes, and Ms. Woods keeps checking
in on Andrew, taking down his thoughts for posterity. I try to make
the apple-nut-raisin cakes in advance for him to offer his teachers. I
leave out a tray with napkins and saucers. I try to keep the apartment
picked up. I line up Andrew's space figures on the windowsill. I guess
Grace Towle is having an influence on me as far as making little
gestures and parts of daily life more, well, aesthetic. I admit there's
something to it, not as much as she may think, but something. I find
some dried hickory leaves, still yellow, and make an arrangement on
the kitchen table.

I decide to start writing down little notes about the boys' childhoods to keep for them. I get a spiral notebook and begin writing a
sentence a night. Anything, like how much Elder weighs now (fifty-
three pounds), how many goals Richie saves for his soccer team, how

ONE WAY HOME

many times Ms. Sowers and Ms. Woods have been by to see Andrew. How many nights The Wrench stays over. It is a quantitative journal, and I feel like some old Puritan merchant gloating over his stores of whale oil. I am hoarding little golden nuggets of detail for them to read about when they are old men. I am sure Andrew, who looks forward to his twilight years, will enjoy it. I am not sure about Richie.

Rich himself never calls to discuss anything. At least not when I am at home. He sends messages, but they are open messages. He swears, the boys report to me—I guess they will always have the air of detectives about them—that he will never take them anywhere again unless I know all about it. They promise they will never go off without asking me. Rich will never camp out on the roof; he will not put a dog up there anymore. Sometimes I see the van on the street, and when I come home, I know he has come in and fixed Andrew's lunch because the kitchen is cleaner than I left it. I do not want to see him, and he goes along with this. I know I'll have to see him, talk to him, at some time, but I keep saying not yet. Maybe at Richie's seventh-grade graduation, when Richie is sure to have a big hand in the program.

I have some more dates with Douglas, of the Elder Home slide-show type. He keeps saying he'll tell us about his life when ours slows down. Yes, he has a past, not as great a past as we have, but it is his, all he has. He enjoyed his childhood very much, thank you, with his grandparents at home and his parents in and out doing constructive things.

The boys feel sorry for him, for not having their life of secrets, kidnappings, the whole Rich deal. The Wrench has his adoption and his exotic mother.

Andrew and Richie get into terrible fights over the past, the details of all the lies they have been part of with Rich, his comings and goings. When Douglas is there and the fights start, he listens carefully, looking as if he were taking notes in a class.

Once, Andrew jumps Richie and beats him in the stomach with hard fast punches, so mean and fast, I am too shocked to grab him. Richie holds him at the elbows and tries to stop the pistons of his fists. "I'm going to bust you in your operation place," he yells into Andrew's face, and that makes Andrew stop.

They never fought like this before. Probably they were too busy plotting out their secret lives, but now, leading more normal lives, they feel free to kill each other. The fights get worse. I am afraid to leave them the way I used to. Instead of their old strategy sessions about how they could live their secret lives, they are divided and carry out ambushes, water battles, and pillow fights. When they hear my key in the door, I can hear them rush to a chair or sofa, and when I walk in, there they sit, red and heaving. "Hi, Mom," they breathe together.

I start writing more in my notebook and have to buy another one. Secretly, in spite of myself, in spite of trying to take a leap of faith and believe the best, I tear up the apartment looking for the note Andrew said they left me, telling me they had gone to the Peaks of Otter. I can't find it, but I refuse to think it never was written.

I cut back on the wine and get down to three glasses a night, which I drink while I listen to Richie and Andrew and pull them apart when they fight. More and more I understand, in a dangerous, frightening way, the feeling Daddy must have prized when he drank. The what-can-I-do-about-things feeling. It scares me into sounding like a staff sergeant yelling about when the tough get going, and getting on the ball. On and on I yell about self-control. None of us sees the joke.

The boys keep shaking out new maps, new versions of the past: "That was the time Dad took us to the mountain for the afternoon, that was the time we picked out the puppies, the first time we saw Dover."

"Who's Dover?"

"He's our dog, the one on the roof. I mean the one who used to have to visit us on the roof. Now he lives in the van. But he liked the roof, he really did. Especially when the sun warmed up the slate, he'd lie there with his nose on his paws and sleep until we told him to come in."

I feel smothered by all these new pasts, but I am trying to accept Rich in an open, divorced way. I know there are people who have friendly divorces. Dr. Towle has a friendly adoption. I never would have believed it, but my divorce is warming up this new period; it's helping me lead a normal, boring life with dates—not that Douglas P. Smathers is boring, not to the new me. No. Douglas is not boring. It is very interesting, in a new kind of way, to have someone, a man, listen to what we all have to say, everything. He promises to shake out the map of his life for us to look at, to "explore" is his word, as he puts his hand in my big hair and shakes my head slowly, looking at me.

I feel as if I were flying, not down to the ground from a rope, but swooping high and low in slanting circles like a swallow. We don't have a sex life yet, but we are getting there. Going steady. Where would we have a sex life anyway? I can't leave the boys alone too long or they might murder each other. But when The Wrench is there, I am beginning to think, I might be able to leave the three of them for short periods of time, which is fine with Grace. So sex is somewhere just over the horizon, getting closer, and I like the old-fashioned pace of it. Slow. Courtship slow.

Last week at Elder Home, Bonnie Parham and Horace Williams were parked in front of the luminous concave TV screen in the front lobby, watching one of the soaps. They were holding hands; their eyes were glued to the life-sized brunette who was evidently saying good-bye to someone we couldn't see on the screen. "You are the best first husband a girl could ever have." Her eyes were happy and teary. He murmured something offscreen that sounded like thank you. Horace and Bonnie seemed to understand "the concept," as Richie calls things, and I saw that I still had a ways to go before I would be able to send such a message to Rich, though I was closer than I ever dreamed possible. For a first husband, Rich was unforgettable.

Andrew yells that Dover wants to come in, not through the window, he's at the door, to play with Elder and Home. Should he let him in?

"Why not," I yell.

XI

*O*n December seventh, the day before Andrew's birthday, Elder is killed. A pickup full of firewood hits her and knocks her over to the side of the street. I don't see it happen, or see her again. She has been buried by the time I hear about it.

Andrew says he came home from school to find his dad waiting for him by his van. He knew something was wrong. Home was lying perfectly still on the cold sidewalk, not moving, as if she were sick. At first, Andrew thought his dad was there to tell him Home had to go to the vet and that Elder was upstairs in the apartment, but no. Elder was dead, in the van, wrapped up in an old blanket, "the blanket we took to the mountains," he says, as if the mountains were where he and Richie used to visit every summer, long years ago when he was a child.

Andrew is not crying, so I ask some questions. He looks as if something had crumpled inside his chest.

"How long had the dogs been out when it happened? Did your dad leave them outdoors by themselves? You gave him a key to the apartment so he could let them out *and* watch them."

"Dad said he let them out ten minutes before it happened and

Elder shot out into the street for no reason, like she was off on a rabbit hunt, but when she was hit, there was not a drop of blood on the street or on the sidewalk, just a little on her tongue. We think she was crushed up inside near her heart. We don't know why she ran in front of the truck. The man felt bad, real bad about it, but there was nothing he could do unless he had turned his truck over or run into all the parked cars. No, Dad didn't leave the dogs by themselves." His voice wavers toward a high whisper.

"Dad wouldn't unwrap the blanket for me to see her because he said I should always think of her as she was, remember her jumping high and singing her dog songs when she saw us coming."

"Where exactly was she hit, I mean, where on the street? Was there any chance of going to the vet?"

"Mom, Elder is dead, face it. It doesn't matter now, does it, all these details? Dad said he saw the whole thing. The pickup slowed down, swerved away from her but hit Elder on her left shoulder hard enough to throw her to the side of the street, right across from the big maple tree. It was all Elder's fault. She ran right out at the truck, acting crazy. Home sat on the sidewalk and watched her. Dad had just turned them out for a ride in the van to the park to go running, his back was turned to open the back of the van, he had told them to sit, and they did. He had parked the van where he always parks on the side street and in those few minutes when he went to open the back doors, everything happened. He ran, but by the time he got to Elder, he says, she was gone. It was instant. He used the word 'gone,' but he meant 'dead.' The driver stopped, he was real sorry, like I just said, but kept saying he couldn't do anything else but hit her."

"What did you do then?"

"I called The Wrench."

"Then what?"

"There wasn't anything to do but wait for you and Richie. I knew Richie would be a little late because of his Christmas play practice, and I knew you were working late, so Dad and I got in the van with Elder all wrapped up and Home lying beside her. Dad and I just sat and waited. It was only about thirty minutes, in fact, it was exactly thirty minutes because I was watching Dad's watch."

"Rich doesn't wear a watch."

"I know. He gave me his dad's pocket watch. He was going to wrap it up for my birthday, but decided to give it to me . . . early. It's gold, or looks like gold, and has trees and mountains engraved on the cover that snaps down over the face. It's almost a hundred years old and only works for thirty minutes at a time. Dad was saving up to get it fixed, but when this happened to Elder he decided to give it to me then. I am supposed to use it half the time and let Richie use it the other half, but I am in charge of it. I held it and watched the time."

"I remember the watch. It's beautiful. What happened then?"

"Richie came home. We got out and waited for him on the sidewalk. Home stayed in the van and put her paws over her nose. I think she was trying to hide her head or her eyes. Like me, Richie didn't cry, but he did have to sit down and put his head down between his legs like he learned to in his first aid class. But when he could stand up, he was okay and listened to Dad tell what happened."

"Then what?"

"Then it was time for Elder to be buried. Dad said we shouldn't come with him, but should take Home inside and brush her and give her a good supper, maybe a shower with shampoo while we waited for you to get home. So that's what we did and he drove away with Elder. We had Home all dry and we cleaned up the water on the bathroom floor before you got home. You didn't even notice the wet towels. Dad decided we shouldn't go with him to bury Elder for three reasons. One, we had all promised you we wouldn't leave again. Two, it was raining by then, almost sleeting. Three, it would be better not to help bury her so we would remember her right—jumping and all those things I told you. Oh, and four, it was a weeknight. So I called The Wrench again and gave him an update."

Andrew reports all this to me when I get home late, around eight-thirty. It is true, I don't even notice the damp bathroom. I am late because we had a Pearl Harbor dinner at Elder Home for all those who had loved ones killed there or who wanted to come to a dinner with flags and "White Christmas" music from old scratched records. Mrs. Osborne was supposed to be in charge of the dinner but changed her mind. "The press of things" was her reason for cutting out on me and leaving me with the whole deal. She didn't want to drive on the icy streets either. She knew I didn't mind, she said. I had called

Andrew but he must have been in the van waiting with his dead dog and Home and Rich. Then later, the boys must not have heard the phone when they were giving Home a bath.

Andrew is dry-eyed, but his voice is the voice of a lost boy who is trying to remember where he took the wrong turn in the woods. Which tree was it where he had put the little notch? I can see the question on his face. He sounds ancient, looks ancient.

Elder was the lively dog, the one who held hands with me by holding my hand in her mouth coming down stairs or walking. It was Elder who could toss the pillows from the sofa onto the floor by nosing under them so fast they flipped off. We called it a trick and told everyone we had taught her to do it. Elder, according to Richie, thought she was a person, or close to one, with favorite colors and places, foods, of course, and television shows. Home liked what her sister liked, but with Elder we always had to "negotiate," Richie said and take her mood into account. Playful and mournful were her two best moods. The Wrench had envied us the dogs, but because he stayed over so much, he felt he had adopted them, only they lived with us.

While I listen to Andrew's report about Elder, I can hear, even under his ancient, sad, lost-boy voice, all the new signs of an honor roll student—none of the old I-need-help-with-this-please that he has used in school since first grade. No, he gives the facts in a clear, organized way. I begin to cry. He doesn't sound all that different from the doctors at Elder Home, who make reports to their pocket dictating machines as they are making rounds, except that his voice is sadder. The Wrench shows up and pats me and calls me by my name, not Mrs. McFall. "Don't cry, Ruth. It's okay."

Richie, who has let his brother do all the talking up to this point, begins patting me on my shoulders, my hair, my face.

"Don't cry, don't cry. It's not your fault. Elder knew not to run in the street. She just forgot, made a mistake. Stop crying, Mom. It won't help her or you. Dad promised Andrew he would find a real pretty place for her grave, out on a farm he knew about, and we could look for a big rock to put on it next week and plant a pine tree. This weekend he thought maybe we could take some pine and cedar branches to put over the grave."

Of course, of course, I am able to say, of course, they can go to

Elder's grave with Rich. Richie has that doctor's voice too, the one that ranges over human history describing suffering and death in a slightly different way, as if they did not matter as much as we might think at the moment, but fit into some long Milky Way of history. The galaxy view, I called it. Dr. Towle has somehow exerted this good influence on the boys.

That night about ten, Douglas comes over. The bad news about Elder makes him sick and his reaction helps us. He doesn't have to put his head down between his knees, as Richie had to do when he heard, but he puts both hands up to his chin and keeps them there the whole time he listens to the story.

"So your father has been letting the dogs out during the day?" Douglas says, his head still clamped down on his fists as we sit at the kitchen table. The boys nod. I nod. It is true, but I don't like to think about it. Douglas says, "That's nice," in exactly the voice Mama used when there wasn't anything else to say. Rachel Marshall and her winter parties were "nice." Then, just like Mama, Douglas says another one of her words for things there weren't many words for. "That's remarkable."

Elder had taken to Douglas first, more than Home. She would climb up on his chest and stare in his eyes until he said, "Kiss me, Dogwoman." Then she would lick his face almost off, but not until he said that. Sometimes he said, "Sing to me, Dog Star," and she would sing in little mournful howls and yips. We loved to see them playing. Home comes over to Douglas and sits by him, then flops down on his feet and tries to hide her eyes. It is a sad evening.

~~~

With all the events in my dating life with Douglas Smathers, and there had been some unusual ones, beginning with the kidnapping and surgery, the absorption of a third child into the menagerie, and now the death of our dog, we have not gotten any closer to sex. Some very nice hugs and kisses. Which is fine with me, fine with him. We are like a very elderly couple, I guess: the feelings are there, but we just can't find the right circumstances, optimum conditions.

Like me, it turns out, Douglas has a past that more or less puts the present on hold. I had thought I was one of the few people with a past that reached out to grab the present and future. Some of the old people at Elder Home have a similar problem, and a side effect— using the past to compete with other people, to one-up them. My past is better than your past. I have done it too. I have thought my life was a little sadder than anyone else's, as if sadness were the measure used for the quality of life. Not that anyone likes or invites sad events, of course. No one asks for a Pearl Harbor or kidnapped children. But once these sad things have happened and they are in the photo album, so to speak, they are something to be secretly proud of. They have cost a lot. Mama used to say "cloudy trophies," and I never knew what she meant. I think I am beginning to.

Douglas tells me more about his past, a sad one, after Elder's death. The boys and The Wrench are out with Rich and his girlfriend, or phantom girlfriend, Pinkie, the one with the horses and, I think, a helicopter. The one who has a farm, where Rich buried Elder. They are celebrating Andrew's birthday by visiting Elder's grave. The apartment is quiet, we are alone.

There was a wife in Douglas's past, his Amelia Colleen, and she died the first year they were married. This was ten years ago. They were twenty-three then. She picked up a staph infection from the hospital where she worked in the operating room, and before they knew it, almost, she was dying, and then dead. Every member of the hospital staff had come to her funeral, all shifts.

Douglas thinks that Amelia's death killed both sets of his grandparents, not at once, but within three years, and his parents. He feels sure, he says, that heartbreak and shock killed them all, even though his parents died in a car accident five years after Amelia died. All the facts gathered by the police only convinced him more that his parents were so distracted by grief even five years later that they drove through the guardrail and fell down the ravine to the river. He couldn't say this, had not had anyone to say it to, and it didn't matter in the long run why they had the accident, really, and he is only guessing. But the accident doesn't to this day make sense. A clear day, no rain, no one else on the road. And then, for no reason, through the rail and turning over and over. For his grandparents, a series of strokes, heart attacks, falls, but he is sure that they gave up when Amelia died and just died or killed themselves. Do I think heartbreak can kill six people? Yes. I point out the obvious, that it was a tribute to Amelia Colleen that her mother-in-law and father-in-law had loved her so much, not to mention the grandparents-in-law.

Douglas says yes, he thinks about that.

He made a decision then, after all the deaths, that he would have to be a different person from the one who had loved and been married to Amelia, a different person from the one who had grown up with his Whitaker and Smathers grandparents, a different person from the one who loved math and computers, if he wanted to go on living. Otherwise, he would die too. Given that basic choice, he became a new person, changed careers from computers to drug education, moved a lot, and now, after ten years, was pretty good at being the Douglas P. Smathers I know. A pharmaceutical company pays him to go to schools and give programs. He doesn't have to mention the name of the company to students. The company writes it off as community service.

I am, he says, Amelia's opposite. I say Amelia must have been wonderful. Douglas agrees. She was that, he says. And I am wonderful too, but in a different way, very different. I point out that I think, so far, that he is the opposite of Rich, and he agrees that it looks that way to him too, though there are things about Rich he likes, admires in many ways. Letting the dogs out for us is one.

I put a stop to the conversation at this point because where is it headed? Back to childhood? Back to when I admired Rich? Will I soon have to agree with Douglas that Rich has some good qualities? So I pick up on the word he was using before he got to Rich being anything.

"Different," I say, is one of those words that can mean anything. So can the word "interesting." I begin telling Douglas how Mama used the word "remarkable" to cover the good, the bad, or the ugly. I knew there was trouble when I heard "remarkable." Does he realize that he uses Mama's words? I am beginning to think I am dating—inadequate word—a man who is very like my mother. I begin to think an old thought, that I had married a man like my father.

"Do you know the expression 'cloudy trophies'?" I ask Douglas late that night at the kitchen table.

He laughs. "It's not exactly an expression, Ruth. It's poetry. Keats."

"Whatever," I say in Andrew's bored voice.

"Sad things become beautiful when they are hung on the walls of memory—I have always thought it meant something like that—and in my case this has been true. I can now think of my past as beautiful, I mean as having moments, long periods of beauty in it, because of the time that has passed, allowing memory to do its work on me and the past. Of course, Keats says it better."

"I doubt it." I sound like the old belligerent Andrew in school to a teacher he wants to notice his learning disability.

"No, really. We'll go to a secondhand book store I know on Granite Avenue and find an old Keats."

For me, this talk of opposites and words and sadness is a romantic conversation, and I really enjoy it except when he gets to the "nice" and "remarkable" things about Rich. Elder's death makes us too sad to be romantic any other way, but it is very nice being together. I love it. I know Richie and Andrew like Douglas, like to have him listen to them, and like the stories they pull out of him. Home listens to Douglas as closely as we do. The Wrench enjoys talking to Douglas too.

His dogs? What dogs were in his past, I want to know. I want to report my findings to the boys. There were enough dogs to satisfy the dog committee, I am sure: a thirteen-year-old St. Bernard named Brandy, a Snowball, a Chub, a Useless, a Bullet, a Bubbles, a Pie, a Smudge, a Big Foot. Bubbles was a three-legged dog. Cancer. Douglas is a dog man, no surprise, but with his job taking him to cities, he can't have a dog. In fact, he argues that pets kept in apartments are prisoners, maybe not quite prisoners, but close. Home has her chin on his knee and is looking up at him as if he were reciting her favorite poem or something. Probably Keats. We laugh at his point about pets being in prisons in apartments. Then he laughs himself and adds, "Pets who live on roofs have more freedom, I guess," which makes Richie and Andrew laugh very hard when I tell them the next morning.

By eleven-thirty, we are telling dog stories to each other. Douglas cranks up the stove and makes grilled cheese sandwiches with corned beef and mustard.

Then we launch into an argument about cats. He is a cat man, too. He has had a Persephone, a Tulip, a Custard, an Oliver, a Falstaff, a Lady Brett, and a Bug in his past too. Cats and dogs don't mix. You can't be a dog person and a cat person, I say. Says who, he yells back, banging his fist on the table. You need a cat here, if you ask me. I don't ask you, I say.

It's eleven forty-five when Douglas says it's time to kiss. I say kiss away, and he does. Maybe grown-up sex or pre-sex is like this, full of jokes and playfulness. If I hadn't been a young person once and didn't know how dead serious sex is for teens, I would think sex for the young was a high-spirited, fun-all-the-way thing. It's not. But this kiss is very fun-loving and filled with promises about the future.

At twelve, the boys have been dropped off and are falling asleep with their heads on Home. All three are piled up with Home in the center of Andrew's bed.

Douglas puts both arms around me to walk down the little hall back to the living room. He doesn't want to talk dogs or cats or sad things. He wants to give me some advice, no charge.

"Shoot." I kiss his cheek. "We are like the old couples at Elder Home. We take our pleasures in the spirit of, I guess, eternity, of why not, the afterlife is waiting just across the bar."

"Just wait, be patient, good things, even sex, happen to good people. I feel that we are going to have a winner of a private life, glorious, if I do say so. But now I want to tell you what I think about Christmas."

"Oh great, now it turns out you are a religious nut. I knew you must have a problem. I know a nurse in Lynchburg who would be perfect for you. Every other word is 'Jesus.' I just couldn't see it in you. Your cooking and calming talents fooled me."

"No, now listen. You have a tendency to think you know what's going to happen, what people are going to say, and I must admit that often you are right, on the money, many times. Many times."

"Yes, I admit, I do have a slight talent in that direction. A kind of a Cassandra. At least, I can feel bad news coming sometimes. However, however, however, I do admit I never thought Elder would be killed. And I never thought the boys would let themselves be kidnapped, or to say it another way, that even Rich would take them off camping, whichever way you want to describe their Halloween night field trip."

"It's very good of you to admit your errors, infrequent as they are. Though they have been stunners—the errors, the bad news. Now I want to propose something to you and turn our thoughts from these sad events. A proposal I want you to think carefully about, promise me."

"Not marriage. I have been married, thank you very much, and I think, so far, anyway, this celibate dating is more what I like as a grown-up."

"No, no, not marriage, not yet, not that kind of proposal. I have been married too, and it was perfect. It's a safe warm room floating through the sky, that's a happy marriage. I feel more and more sure ours could be a room, maybe an apartment or house floating in the sky, but as I said, I am not, at this point, definitely not, proposing."

"There is no need to be so emphatic. I get your drift. You are not proposing." Here we had a nice long kiss, movie quality.

"What I want to suggest to you is this. Invite Rich and his Pinkie over for Christmas dinner. The boys and Home would be happy, and I would like to meet this myth of a man, very much, in fact. It's hard to compete with a man on a roof, a man in the frozen past, a one-of-a-kinder."

I jerk away from my embrace and flop down on the sofa, my late-night pleasure bubble vanishing into the lamplight.

"No way. You invite him over to your place, and sure, take Richie and Andrew. Invite the doctor and The Wrench. You can go after the school play to make sure Richie and Andrew don't run off to the mountains again, or you can have them over Christmas Day, or you can all go to this Pinkie's estate and ride horses or fly airplanes. But please, dear Jesus, leave me out of your plans. When I am around Rich, I mean, around where he has been, just the air even, I feel a mental sickness come on."

"I think I know how you feel. Not exactly, maybe not even close, but something about how you feel. Trust me, I have thought and thought about this and I think it's a good plan to have a family, in the new sense, get-together. Rich is always going to be part of your life, not to mention the boys', and, I hasten to add, I hope that he will be part of my life. I want to meet him. In short, invite the ex-husband

of all ex-husbands to Christmas dinner for my sake if not for yours or
the boys'."

"Your sake would be the only sake at this dinner—if I should be
crazy enough to go along with it—I would be thinking of."

"That's good. I knew you would think about it, Ruth. I know you
will think hard about it this week."

"Well, that much I can promise you. I will think about it hard. But
one thing is for sure, for damn sure. Rich and Pinkie or Bluey or
whatever her name is, if there is such a person, are not ever going to
be *invited* here. Maybe Rich can bring her in the old roof way
through a window, but he's not coming in the front door, with me
running down the steps to let him and this Pinkie in."

"But Rich has a key, remember—he let the dogs out for a run every
day."

"And look what happened!"

"Now, you know that Elder was not killed because of Rich."

"Well, in a way, it was cause and effect."

"Who gave Rich the key?"

"I let Richie give it to him. I wouldn't answer him when he asked
for it, but I was glad he did ask. Not answering meant yes, I admit
that."

"And you admit that all Rich has done is let out the dogs, I mean,
now it will be just dog, Home, out. You don't mind his cooking in your
kitchen occasionally, do you?"

"Yes, you are right. I mind and I don't mind." I pause and then ask,
"Why are those words—'You are right'—a man's favorite words,
much more than 'I love you,' or 'I am undressing' or 'Here is a million
bucks'?"

Douglas is laughing at me. "What about Elder Home?"

"What about it?"

"Would you consider inviting Rich and his Pink Lady to Christmas
dinner there?"

"Look, it's late. You must be tired, overworked, or hanging around
us too much. Go home. Dream about your past, your sad, sad past
with Amelia in the safe room up in the sky. Just don't strain my
nervous system with such thoughts as Rich in an old people's home.
He is the opposite of old people in every way, and this Pinkie must
be too."

"I think it would be very nice to have dinner there and maybe Richie would put on his school play there, at least say his part of the play for your people after dinner."

"Well, I think it would be very horrible, the whole thing. For one thing, Mrs. Osborne charges an arm and leg for holiday meals because she knows that's the only time guests come and there are no restaurants close by, so she has them and charges up to eight-fifty a plate for canned turkey, canned peas, canned cranberry jelly. Canned apple pie."

Douglas is laughing at the canned pie. He kisses my cheek. We are an old couple again, beyond the dangers of a sex life. Suits me. I am mad at this person who gives such dumb advice out of the blue. He is still laughing when he gets his coat on. Then he grabs me and in a not-so-old way, kisses me good-bye, and whispers in my ear that he loves the thought of canned pie.

I sit down to begin writing a letter to Mama. I'm too upset to sleep, and it's been two months since I wrote, and her letters have been lost, at least I haven't seen them. They probably got caught up in the piles of homework papers Andrew thrashed through as an invalid. As I write, my life unfurls like a sail and I see in my own handwriting that my sons have been in school programs, had a good beginning of a soccer season, had some teachers over, have been camping, had an appendectomy with no complications—I slide Andrew's operation in on page three—that went very well, acquired two dogs, though one was killed, which was very sad. We have made friends with two nice adults, a doctor and an educator (I leave out any reference to drugs). Andrew and Richie have a new friend, the son of the doctor, who is brilliant and fun to be with. He is called The Wrench. We are all planning a Christmas party. On paper, my life looks so good that I send love to James and his Sarah, Marianne, and Elinor. I want to write about my dream of finding a house where Mama's electric wheelchair can come and go. We'd have ramps at every doorsill.

Mama will notice first thing that my address is an old one for me. She wants me to have a permanent address, not the stamped red hand pointing to *Forward*. It will make her happy just to see my return address is still the same. She will say, "Remarkable."

XII

A week later, Andrew, The Wrench, and Richie work on making invitations to the Christmas dinner at Elder Home on
December 21.

I have been thinking hard about Douglas's bad idea to invite Rich
to Christmas dinner, Rich with his Pinkie friend, and I decide, Why
not. I don't want to look as if I were the only one with a problem.

The boys think a big Christmas party is a great idea. It can make
up a little for the sad birthday Andrew had, and Douglas goes up
higher on their scale of cool. They are not surprised that he has a past
in computers; they, of course, have known it longer than I have.

"That's how he thought up this Christmas deal with Dad," Andrew
says. "He's a computer brain." This is the highest praise I've ever
heard.

Andrew wants Ms. Woods, who is still calling him to check on his
readjustment to the classroom, to come to our party too. Richie wants
Ms. Vincent invited. Andrew and The Wrench start calling it "our
party" or "the party." I try to slow them down some, reminding them
that teachers have their own families, it is short notice, teachers have
their own plans for their own Christmases. But The Wrench points

out that our party will be more interesting than any teacher's. Andrew agrees. Richie says *that* is a good point.

The boys do not ask me why out of the blue we are inviting Rich
to dinner. They act as if it were a normal thing. They act as if I didn't
have a history of avoiding Rich, of moving from town to town, apartment to apartment, and of trying to avoid him for them too. So, I
begin to try to act normal too, mainly because it is so painful to be the
odd one out in a family, the one wet blanket.

It takes The Wrench to explain to me what is happening in my
emotional life, and once I resign myself to the outrage of listening to
the wisdom of a ten-year-old, even one with an IQ of 147, I can take
in his point. He, too, it seems, knows what it means to feel like a
"monkey wrench" in the plans of beloved people. He, too, knows
what it means to screw up things for people. His whole life tells that
little story. His asthma tells another version of that story—asthma
makes things more difficult, things that are already difficult. I find
myself nodding in agreement as if I were listening to a grown person,
to his mother, the adopted one. His counseling technique must have
come from her. But, he goes on, he has made a discovery.

"A wrench, you know, does not have to be a monkey wrench. It can
fix things." This is his great wisdom. Andrew nods wisely and falls
over backward laughing. Richie falls on top of him, not trying to avoid
the operation place. Home jumps on top. I feel as if I should do
something physical, so I hug The Wrench in a modern, fuzzy-wuzzy
way, and say, half meaning it, "You are brilliant! Almost obnoxious
at times, many times."

"I know. It comes with the territory." He smiles.

Andrew's invitation to his father and Pinkie is a picture of a rocket,
going straight across the paper.

"Don't rockets go up in the sky?" I want to know.

"Not always—some blast off sideways. Space is not just up,"
The Wrench notes. The rocket is a deadly-looking weapon except
colored a sunset pink, very precise in its rocket details. The letter
part is squeezed onto the rocket body and curves down toward the
tail. He has room only for the facts. XMAS DINNER. DEC 21, ELDER HOME.
Then he signs his name in the fuel exhaust smoke. I ask him if he
thinks a rocket and Christmas go together and he just looks at me,

asking in silent eye-talk where have I been for the last fifty thousand years.

Richie's invitation is a real letter:

> Dear Dad,
>   Would you like to come to Christmas dinner with Andrew and me? The Wrench whom you have met will be there with his mother, Dr. Grace Towle, if she can trade duties with someone at Memorial Hospital. We will eat at Elder Home. You know where it is. Mom will be there and our friend Douglas P. Smathers. Please ask Pinkie if she can come. We are going to ask Mom's boss if we can bring Home to the party. Thanks for the new leash. We will use it at the party. Thanks for driving us out to Elder's grave. It was very pretty.
>
>   Love,
>   Your Son
> P.S. I did what you suggested.
> P.S.S. It's on Dec. 21. Can you bring the tree?

I get to read the rocket letter and the real letter by twisting my neck around and walking backward as I fix supper.

"Mom, you're going to hurt yourself. Just ask." Richie is copying his letter over, so I can see his more plainly. He says I can read his "rough draft" and puts it in my hand.

"Too easy. Mom likes a challenge. Don't hand her your letter." Andrew is outlining the rocket in black. "She can read upside down. She can read with her eyes shut, especially if it has anything to do with you know who."

"May I read your letters? With my eyes open and right side up. I do not have ESP about you know who." I am hurt. "Who told you to ask Rich to bring the tree? What did you do that your father suggested?"

"You don't need to read our letters now. I can see you breaking your neck to see what we have written. I don't write any secrets. You know I want to ask Pinkie to come. You'll like her. She's different."

"Good, maybe she's different enough to land on the roof of Elder Home in her helicopter. Or maybe she doesn't need a helicopter. Anyway, remember it was my idea, I think, to have this Christmas party, at least, more than yours."

"Mom, Pinkie has a pilot's license. She does not own a helicopter. I don't know why you have to add 'helicopter' every time her name comes up."

"Every single time." Andrew is using a blue crayon with the paper skinned off to make a sky for his rocket. He puts the crayon down flat and makes a sky that has texture, different blues and whites embossed in a few swoops across the page.

"Okay, I'll call her the pilot from now on and not mention the helicopter."

"Dad doesn't call Douglas the drug man."

"What does he call him?"

"Your mom's friend, that's all I ever heard him say."

"Look, let's change the subject. I was wondering, Dr. Richie, if you would like to adapt your school program, part of it, for my people at Elder Home? Or you could write something new for them. Maybe a poem."

"All my plays are about drugs. Do they need to know about drugs?"

"Some of them know more about drugs than any other subject, but maybe you could lighten up a little with them. Try something new."

"But they want to know all the bad stuff."

"They do know it all, a lot of it anyway, so I thought a little lightness would be good for them, Christmas and everything. Write about yourself. You were right, in your letter, to think of a tree. We need a tree, and we certainly don't have one. Mrs. Osborne says an artificial tree works fine, the one she has put up for the past century, ratty-looking and silver. If we get a real tree, at no cost, and at no trouble, she'll love it. I mean she'll like it."

Andrew is working on another rocket. "We think ahead, Mom. You're in good hands with us." He says his next rocket is for Grammer in Illinois. She sent him twenty dollars in one-dollar bills when he was recovering from his operation and for his birthday, and he has not written to her to thank her, so his rocket, he thinks, can deliver two messages. Ms. Woods's invitation he can do at school. There's plenty of time in class, he says. Everyone has a secret project to do in class.

"Grammer can't come, won't be able to come. She's in a wheelchair. By the time your rocket gets there, she'll have maybe forty-eight hours to get a ticket and fly here."

"So? She'll like my thoughts." He keeps on working on his pink rocket, adding spirals. Even on the envelope he puts smoke and stars, leaving space around Grammer in Illinois's address. I say why not include his first cousins, Elinor and Marianne, in the invitation, his uncle and aunt, too, since none of them can come. He says it's not a bad idea, even though he doesn't know what they look like. He would like to know what his uncle looks like. He thinks he remembers Grammer from when he was four, he's not sure. I say that's right. She came to see him and Richie to say good-bye when she was leaving to go live with Uncle James and Aunt Sarah in Illinois. Andrew can't remember James at all. He would like to meet his kin people, he repeats twice. I say it's a good idea, a very good idea, but how about after Christmas.

The Wrench adds his two cents to Andrew's monologue: Family is very important. He enjoys both his adopteds and his biologs. He gets twice the number of presents for every birthday, and sometimes, if his adopted has time, she gives him a half-birthday.

Andrew's eyes widen. "A what?"

"Half-birthdays are celebrated exactly six months from the real ones. Mine, for example. My birthday comes on September sixteenth, but that's a bad time for birthdays, when you think about it. School has just started. It's not summer and it's not cold weather. It's in between seasons, like a marsh is not dry land or river. I don't like it. I forget the other bad reasons for my birthday. Anyway, on March sixteenth, I have a party every year. March is the worst time for anything, so if you can think of any excuse for a party, you should. I always enjoy this half-party. You can have one on June eighth."

I interrupt the world's expert on half-birthdays and get Andrew and Richie to return to the subject of family life.

"Well, you are inviting your dad for this Christmas and Pinkie, a *pilot*. That will have to hold you on the family thing for a while. You say Pinkie is nice, and that I will like her because she is interesting and not a show-off."

"You know you hate people to show off, like teachers do, to act big, in other words. Pinkie is nice and acts, I guess you would have to call it, little instead of big."

At Elder Home, when I ask Mrs. Osborne about the party and about bringing Home and my five, maybe six or seven if the teachers come, other guests, Ozone Level goes into her usual routine. She says she'll have to take it up with the Board. Giving a family party—that's what it boils down to—at Elder Home is in fact using the premises for other than official purposes and must have approval of the Board.

I tell her I will be organizing the Christmas party for the residents and their families anyway, doing all the work—I slip that killer in—and at the most will have only seven guests (not counting the dog). I add that I thought open houses at Christmas, Yule drop-ins, were meant for outsiders, guests. The more the merrier. Decked halls, wise men, children, gifts, holly and ivy.

No, I am mistaken. Of course the Board does want community involvement when it is, in fact, real community involvement, not when it is, in fact, a private affair. Certainly using the facility for personal things, for family life that should be lived at home, is not what the Board would want. Why, if every member of the staff decided that it would be nice to have a family reunion or little get-together . . . why, surely I could understand the position I would be putting the administration and Board in.

At this point, I promise to work New Year's Eve and every weekend during the bad-weather months when the streets are icy. So the party is set. Ozone Layer almost says no to Home's coming, but I remind her that we had a pet fashion show in August, which was her idea and I add, one of the best activities, if not *the* best. Home would not be the first animal to visit.

Special events and activities are miracles to me, considering the way Ozone interferes and puts up roadblocks.

"I'm getting smarter, about my career, about supervisors, bosses." I am telling Douglas about the improvement in my attitude as a member of the work force of the nation, a dull subject even to me. "I help Mrs. Ozone look good, I let her advise and correct me, I let her seem to straighten out problems I have caused. Then I thank her. Then I thank her again. It works. I think I am applying what The Wrench told me about fixing things. He makes it seem a little too simple, though."

As the party, our party, looms closer, we are busy plaiting grape-vine wreaths and popping corn for the strings of cranberries and popcorn. I have been cleaning the roof garden at Elder Home and fixing up the old ballroom that opens onto the roof garden. The building was an Eastern Star/Masonic building—*1911* is cut in the cornerstone—with secret meanings designed into the fancy brickwork. The women had many formal affairs—gowns, orchestras—and the roof garden, I have heard, was quite a lovely place. Now, of course, its corners are filled up with soot and trash that blows over the city, the wrought-iron railing over the brick wall is rusting, and the television antenna is hanging off the far corner. Douglas helps me sweep and shovel up twenty big bags of trash after he gets off work.

The boys report that Rich and his Pinkie are looking for the biggest tree on her farm. It will have to come up the fire escape outside. We are making all-natural decorations. Suet balls, seed strings.

"Yes, and as Mom waves her arms," Andrew is saying to Douglas, "Canada geese will land in formation and politely eat our popcorn." Richie is in charge of popping pan after pan of popcorn. The Wrench is now spending almost every night with us to help get ready for our party. We string what we can at night and I take in big bags full of popped corn for the volunteers to string with the residents. We sing carols while we string, and Sallie Larkin, a ninety-two-year-old, plays the piano. Sometimes she changes carols midway through and we finish "The First Noel" with "Hark, the Herald." Sallie used to come to Elder Home as an Eastern Star in evening dress. She talks about dancing on the roof.

"Isn't this messy," Ozone Layer always says as she walks through the activities room, picking her feet up high, as if she's afraid that the popcorn will stick to her.

"Canada geese are too big. They might collapse the roof or scare everyone into the midnight clear. I am inviting starlings, city birds, to fly down, hover, and eat a berry and kernel. Like little sea gulls." The Wrench sounds confident that he can summon certain birds to our party. No one doubts him. He has explained to us the distress call he has mastered and the screech owl call that will bring birds from all over almost to his hand.

The Wrench has another guest he would like to invite. Officer Armentrout, we will remember, the one who helped him when he wrecked his bike, well, he has no family, no regular family, just prisoners, who can be nice people if you choose them carefully. One of his prisoner friends just finished college. They are not all murderers.

"Go on, girl," says Andrew. "I remember that state trooper, he was cool, him and Alonzo Johnson, whose hand was broken and your mom fixed it. Did Alonzo finish college?"

"Not Dr. Johnson. He's not going to college. No, he gets in too many fights. You will remember that's why he is called Doctor—the opposite of what he is. Just like me."

"Say what?"

"My name is the opposite of me."

"Yeah, and my name is just Andrew."

"What name would you like, what nickname? It has to relate to you in some way. Mine is my opposite. I mean I started life as a monkey wrench, ruining my biological mom's plans, but I ended up being a wrench that fixes things, her life, too. She doesn't know what she'd do without me to write to and think about."

Andrew wants a name that connects him to rockets or dogs. The Wrench says that will take some thought, an expression Andrew has picked up from him.

Douglas asks if this roof garden place will really work for our party. It looked pretty bad, "cheesy," Richie said, the last time he was up there. Douglas and Andrew had gone up there for Sallie Larkin. She wanted someone to bring her back a description, and Douglas said he'd be happy to do it. Andrew offered to go along. He and Douglas agreed after some thought not to tell Sallie Larkin how filthy the roof was.

That's when I started cleaning it every day at lunch, as well as later when Douglas got there.

I ask Richie not to use the word "cheesy." He points out that I use "baloney" and "hot dog."

" 'Baloney' and 'hot dog' are classic American words." Douglas speaks in his expert's voice. It's great to have a resident expert. I like having a champion around who makes me feel like Guinevere, and I say so. All of a sudden, The Wrench slaps his head and whispers to Andrew, who thinks a minute and then speaks deliberately.

"Call me Champ. It's a double nickname, short for champion, and the opposite of me, in a way. I mean I went to the hospital and I am the youngest, so I am not exactly a champion . . . yet, anyway." Andrew's voice is very expert too. We all shake hands as if we were at the end of a medieval christening service.

"You know, Andrew"—Douglas is as solemn as stone—"it takes a long time for people to get used to calling someone by a new name. Don't expect us to always call you by your new name."

"I won't," he answers. "I know that I am Andrew, too."

I try to change the subject, back to the modern era. "I have washed the big glass doors so we can see out of them, and with the big tree out there, we can sit or wheel up close and see the birds flying down to get some treats. We'll have the ballroom decorated with pine branches and—"

"Like the ones on Elder's grave?"

"Just like those. We'll have punch, that white grape juice champagne, and music, real live music, if I can find a group to play for fourteen dollars, and we'll have Richie's program."

"Speaking of that, Mom, I need you to get red gloves for all the old people who will have parts to say. Actually it's more of a poem-play. It calls for a lot of hand action, clapping and snapping fingers, or tapping their canes. Sound effects can be used to bring out meaning, you know. I need some bells, too. All my speakers need a little strap of bells to wear on their wrists, or maybe to keep in their laps until I signal them."

"Go on, girl," Champ says as he slides into a moonwalk. "I'll rap my part." Richie smashes a handful of popcorn in his face and drags him out of the kitchen to beat him up in the living room. The Wrench follows and soon the violence stops.

"No blood on the furniture," Douglas says.

Douglas drove the boys out to Pinkie's farm to help pick out the tree, but really, he said, he wanted to meet Rich before the Elder Home party. When he gets back, I say, "Well, was he like I said he was. Terrible?"

"Not exactly. Your stories don't seem to match the person I met. He took us on a tour of his different garden plots—he's got each garden mapped out already—the spinach and onions, lettuce and radishes for early planting, the potato plot ready to go on St. Patrick's Day, the late garden of turnips and winter squash. Quite impressive, really."

"What did he look like up close?"

"As if he'd been through a couple of wars. No, not too bad, not as bad as you said he looked. Mild, really."

"All I can say is that you didn't meet the Rich I was married to."

"Probably not. Remember that I am not the Douglas who was married to Amelia Colleen. Are you Ruth McFall, Rich's fleeing wife or Ruth Activities or Ruth with friends, in short, Ruth with a new life?"

I can't think of a better answer than "Shut up," a favorite expression of Daddy's when he got in a corner.

～～～

Our personal family gathering Christmas party starts at three o'clock, December 21. I am reunited with Rich and the past, if a wave can be said to reunite with itself; I mean, "reunion" is inadequate for what happens. Did Lee and Grant get together after Appomattox? Here is the man I have been running away from for six years, on the street in front of Elder Home carrying a Christmas tree my "date" is helping him with. The children I had with this man are standing there with their friend, happy as can be.

Getting the tree from Pinkie's farm would have been much easier, and so would lowering it to the roof garden, if she really had owned a helicopter, but then I wouldn't have gotten to see Rich and Douglas wrestling with the tree to get it off the top of the van and up the fire escape.

The boys and I stand with Pinkie on the street and watch the tree begin its climb to the top. Rich had lashed it to the top of the van, and it takes thirty minutes to get it off and started up the fire escape. And, as I say, Rich waves to me. There is no time to talk, and nothing to say. The residents are waiting for the tree to appear. I had promised them by four at the latest and they have been ready since right after lunch, in their red gloves and sparkle-sprayed sheets draped over their shoulders.

Mrs. Ozone Layer thinks old people want to have everything prepackaged—voilà, here, an instant party. That's not true. Oldies like to help get ready for things, and the harder and longer the preparations, the better.

So at three-thirty the tree begins climbing up the side of Elder Home, Rich and Douglas invisible in the long arms of a twenty-five-foot Douglas fir. The tree seems to be moving by itself.

As we are standing on the street watching the tree climb the building, Officer Armentrout's car drives by. He stops, smiles, and says he appreciated the invitation to the party. He is sorry, but he is emceeing a prison party, one he has promised Alonzo all year he'd do. Parties in prison always have to have an emcee, it's a tradition. He waves broken-like fingers to remind us who Alonzo is, not that we have forgotten. He would like to hear about our party, though, and he knows we'd like to have the lowdown on the prison talent show. If it goes well, Alonzo wants to start having prison talent shows for interested citizens to come to. Dr. Johnson has asked to be remembered to us. We had made an impression on him. Then Officer Armentrout drives off, flashing his red lights as a holiday greeting.

When Douglas and Rich get near the top of the steps with the tree, we rush inside and run up the five flights to the roof garden. Sixty red-gloved residents are in the ballroom waiting for us. The glass doors are shining clear from the ammonia baths I have given them. The residents can see the tip of the tree through the doors, and I fling them open as the big fir crests and then topples in the air just beyond the balcony.

They are wrapped up in so many coats and blankets under the sparkled sheets that the cold air feels good for the few minutes it takes to hoist the tree over the balcony and into the barrel we have waiting, half-full of wet sand.

When the tree comes into full view, the residents applaud with their red gloves and begin jingling their little bell straps. I prop the glass doors open, and Rich—the one I knew, not the new mild one—jumps up on the balcony's narrow iron rail, as I was sure he would, and does a cat walk for us five stories up. Which of course everyone but me loves, and they jingle and jingle and clap.

Douglas acts like a grown-up and just waves to the circles of old people. They like him, too, and clap for him. Walking on a rail or waving, it doesn't matter to them. Any walking is miraculous. It's a party that's getting off to a good start.

I see Andrew eyeing the rail and give him a hard punch on his shoulder to show I know what he is thinking about. "No way, Champ," I say. Of course, he falls down and rolls around, Home comes over and licks his face, but Rich, the new one, says, "Get up, son."

Propped up in the barrel with bags of wet sand next to it, the tree is White House caliber.

"Is it legal to have this old-fashioned means of escape?" Pinkie asks me, pointing to the rusting fire steps. "No one here, except us, could escape."

These are the first direct words Pinkie has said to me, not counting a friendly wave with Rich's when the van drove up with the tree. I had waved back, wiggling three fingers and nodding my head slightly, as a foreigner, an exchange person who needs an interpreter, would do. We had not spoken to each other on the street as we watched the tree go up the fire escape—too much to see to talk, I guess.

A word about Pinkie Goforth's accent. Richie had told me she was a foreigner. Andrew said she wasn't foreign, she was French.

I ask her what she is, where she is from. "All over" is her answer. She is easy to listen to and interesting to look at, not in the usual sense. Not a beauty like Phyllis, not a wild Indian like I used to be, not a polished-apple healthy kind of pretty like Grace—like nothing I have seen so far in Richmond. There are nice smile wrinkles around the eyes; she wears no makeup, has short curly hair and blue eyes, plain and calm as plates. I can't believe someone so uncrazy-looking is associating with Rich. Letting him garden on her farm, I guess live on her farm, with her, maybe. Definitely, maybe. I can't decide. She cut the tree herself. Yes, she has a Christmas-tree farm, horses not helicopters, and a big run-down farmhouse, which she would like very much for me to visit with the boys, Douglas, and Home. She would love for The Wrench to bring his mother out, but she knows her schedule must be hectic. She knows my schedule is as difficult. Rich stands there listening and nodding to her words just the way Andrew does when The Wrench is explaining something to us. Rich is friendly, nice, not the Rich I had known.

"That would be nice," I say. Richie adds, "Very nice."

Douglas and Rich begin tamping the wet sand down around the tree in the drum and soon it stands straight. Not even the brisk winds sway it. Then they anchor the drum with wire to the rails of the balcony. We have all the ropes of popcorn and cranberries ready to wrap around the tree.

Not one of the residents slumps over from fatigue. They watch and wave directions to us as we work on the tree. "Higher," they say with their canes. I have closed the glass doors and they tap the glass. "More at the top," they make us understand. I open the glass doors occasionally, worrying if the cold air is too much, but they signal for me to open them up again.

Mrs. Ozone comes by and says to Pinkie that she has been planning our Christmas party for months and is looking forward to seeing her at the special dinner that night. Good manners are everywhere. She turns to me to say a Dr. Towle has called to say she had an emergency and cannot come to the party but will see us at my apartment and pick up her son, she hopes, unless it gets too late. Ozone doesn't mind taking messages from doctors, even personal messages.

Rich and I do not talk to each other, but on the other hand, we do not *not* talk. We talk to other people right next to each other and there is nothing that has to be said directly. I guess if there had been a fire we would have spoken, but there is no fire.

Rich is, as Douglas had said, mild, a milder version, a diluted version, of himself. There is something of the health nut look to him, as if he had stopped bad habits, but a little too late, and taken up good ones that made him feel good but couldn't bring back youth. Pinkie has all her looks in her quiet voice and good manners. She can laugh at the birds pecking away, at Home standing at the glass door and yearning after the birds. "Do you miss your sister?" I hear her say to Home, who appears to answer her.

"I understand your mother was going to try to come to the party and for Christmas." Pinkie's Frenchy voice has a holiday lilt to it.

I hear myself explaining that Mama has written and will be coming in the spring in warmer weather and will stay awhile, I hope.

"Oh yes," Pinkie says.

It is time for Richie's red glove "theater piece"—his words. He does not want to call it a play, when really it is more of a poem or rap with accompanying claps and shouts and taps. He has been coming to practice his "chorus," and it was his idea to drape sheets over the residents in toga fashion to show up the red gloves. Andrew thought of the spray sparkle. The Wrench has written a poem too.

Each wheelchair has a small bough of pine tied to one handle. Some have the cedar with blue berries.

I have not heard Richie's theater piece. A surprise, Andrew says. He is in charge of lights. There's just one switch, I say. On-off, that's it.

169

"Be a dreamer," he says mysteriously.

I should have known he would persuade Ms. Sowers to come. She has brought a fancy light, a spotlight with a color disc of all shades. Ms. Woods surprises us by coming at the last minute. She brings her home movie camera and says she is arranging for Andrew to get extra credit in his social studies.

"For what?"

She looks at me for a moment as if I were the wicked stepmother and she the visiting fairy godmother.

"For all this," Ms. Woods says, sweeping her arms up at my angel-hair ceiling and cedar swags, the mistletoe bunches looping down low with red ribbons. Rich and Pinkie had shot the mistletoe down with her grandfather's twenty-gauge shotgun.

Andrew steps up and says in a new voice, "Mom did all the work. The Wrench and I did give her some advice about the cloudy stuff and the birdseed, and we scattered it on the roof garden. The sheets were my brother's idea, I think."

"Andrew, you're under mistletoe!" Ms. Woods plants a kiss on my ocean-eyed boy, who ducks, but not before she gets him good.

"Call me Champ, please. I have a new nickname."

"It's perfect, too, and fits you exactly, I think. The way you have improved in your cognitive skills is quite remarkable. I would say you have a very good nickname." Ms. Woods tries to kiss him again.

Then she turns back to me, and because I am near the mistletoe or because I am kin to her favorite student, she launches into how much Andrew has improved since his operation. She thinks the individual attention has helped him, as well as the peer tutoring, even though The Wrench is older and not exactly a peer. The Wrench does not have many "peers," anyone who knows him knows that. But, back to Andrew, she says. She enjoys more than she can explain to me Andrew's sense of the world. He seems to understand how it really works. That is the closest she can come.

Richie appears, wrapped up in a red blanket. He has shot sparkle in his hair, which is spiked all around his head. All the residents are very quiet all of a sudden. Their practices in the afternoons give them an assured professional air.

Only Mrs. Warren, who is tied into her wheelchair under her

sparkling sheet "costume," keeps talking. "I am so glad I am still on my feet," she says sweetly. She loves to say this as she leans into the harness that straps her upright in her wheelchair. She says it only once, and then the program begins.

Andrew cuts the lights off, draws the heavy draperies across all the windows except the doors that frame the tree, then turns a spotlight on Richie. He is standing on a stepladder in the corner.

> "Welcome one, welcome all,
> Welcome to our hollied hall.
> We are here and you are here!
> Love, friendship, dogship, cheer!
> Let us all tell a story
> Not of great deeds or of glory,
> Just a simple little story,
> Of a time before this life
> In Elder Home.
> Now, first we start with Mrs. Green,
> Who was born in 1919.
> A very goddess of a very queen,
> Or like my Mama, she's la bamba."

Here Richie points to Mrs. Green, who has never spoken to anyone at Elder Home after the first week, when she wept all day and all night, then fell into a blank silence. Her children come once a week, but nothing doing, she will not speak. Richie waves his wand, which he produces from under his robes, touches her, and Mrs. Green begins.

> "I came here against my will.
> I was not sick, nor was I ill.
> It's not as bad as it could be.
> It's not as good as it should be.
> I guess I'll stay. I have no say."

She smiles, another first. There is a small pounding of red hands and jingling of bells. She bows her head like a famous pianist, slightly, but pleased.

Richie turns to several other residents I did not know had poetry in their souls nor, like Mrs. Green, the ability to speak. More applause. It is clear that he has interviewed each one and written their stories into little raps and gotten them to memorize words. He lip-syncs with them, supplying lyrics when they fade. It is, as Andrew says, super incredible.

Then he turns to Andrew, who goes to the front of the crowd with Home.

> "Here am I and here's my dog.
> Let it snow, let it fog.
> Nothing keeps us from having fun,
> From making our own little sun.
> Maybe you have heard of my operation.
> I'll tell you every detail-ation,
> Of how I felt a sudden cramp
> While camping at a mountain camp,
> But hey, it gave me my new name . . . CHAMP!
> But after cookies, after punch,
> Come see my dog munch-munch.
> My dog once had a sister,
> She got killed."

Andrew doesn't try to rhyme the last lines. His face is very solemn, and Home sits by him, solemn as an oak tree too, except she has sparkle sprayed all over her already-glistening clean black coat and a big red plaid bow on her collar, which has slipped, so she looks cockeyed, more than usual.

The Wrench's turn comes. I expect a Shakespearean sonnet at the very least, but it is a simple nursery rhyme that picks up its theme and rhythm, what there are of them, from Andrew's.

> "I'm here too. My name's The Wrench.
> I help people in a pinch.
> It is true, uh-huh, I have asthma.
> Don't worry, don't need no plasma.
> Once I broke my collarbone.
> I like, uh-huh, to talk on the phone.
> I like for things to come in twos,
> Moms, friends, arms, and shoes."

Here The Wrench opens his arms in a wide victory hug motion. Those residents who can, raise their arms back.

"But sometimes, things work out wrong,
There's only a ding, not a dong,
There's only a ping, not a pong,
Still, still, still we must, uh-huh, sing our song."

Home looks up at The Wrench and lifts her head as if she is going to break into a howling song. But she doesn't, she just looks at him and yawns. There is a big applause, not loud, because clapping arthritic fingers is painful, but a soft, fingery applause fills the ballroom.

Then the mood brightens, and Home does her part by catching a cookie Andrew tosses high in the air. Everyone jingles. We have cookies and punch. Richie has rigged up with Andrew's and The Wrench's help some red and green revolving lights that wheel over the glass doors and the room. The lights can be lifted off the hook and hand-held for close-ups and special effects. There is a lot of taking the lights down and up to certain people and areas of the party. Then he puts on the tapes of the "White Christmas" songs, the same ones we used for the Pearl Harbor party—I couldn't find a group to play for fourteen dollars—and we push the wheelchairs in a kind of samba line around the ballroom.

Mrs. Osborne asks Rich to dance, which he does, turning red and green as he swoops her around the big room, not knocking into anything.

Outside on the tree, a light snow is falling, like fog, as if Andrew's poetry had called it down. Birds are enjoying the popcorn. My headache is somewhere up above the tree, not inside my head any longer. Douglas tells me he thinks it would be nice if he asked Pinkie to dance, and it is true that with Rich off mambaing-sambaing with Ozone, there are no other men on their feet.

"Fine," I say as I swirl away with Richie, Home, Andrew, and old Mr. Merriwether in his motorized wheelchair. Mr. M&M, as we call him, keeps saying, "We're having a ball, we're having a ball, aren't we!" The Wrench pushes Mrs. Warren around to the music. She smiles and says how glad she is to be on her feet. Then he gives Sallie Larkin a ride.

Andrew wants me to know as we wheelchair-dance that Mrs. Herbert is taking her teeth out.

"As long as she doesn't drop them," Richie hisses at him, as if

Andrew were trying to make trouble. He isn't, I can tell. He just doesn't know Mrs. Herbert likes to do that when she is relaxed and having fun.

Someone, I think Ozone, starts changing partners, swinging backward, handing people on their feet and in chairs to each other in crisscrosses and zigzags to the music, like the old Paul Jones dances we used to do in the gym on Fridays to mix up the nondancers with the show-off dancers. A modified fox-trot that I learned at Rachel Marshall's house three million years ago.

Rich gets to me and we both stop dead, a foot apart. The crazy lights are giving us glows of red and greens. He holds his hands out to me, waiting, I guess, to see what I'll do. Walk off the floor? Run away again?

What we do is dance the way we never had a chance to when we were not-dating, when we had our place in the woods, the way he danced with Phyllis when they went out to the proms and I waited to hear about it. It's over in a minute. Mrs. Osborne must have gotten a bad partner and wanted to move on. Rich has time to say he hopes I won't move this time. I have time to say I don't plan to for the time being. He squeezes my hand.

When we change partners I hear Mrs. Herbert say with her teeth in that there is a nice family on the floor. Andrew says back to her, "They're mine."

"Which ones, dear, which ones are yours?" She removes her teeth with a little excuse-me-please cough. "Point them out to me."

Andrew uses his spotlight to point us out, changing from red to green and back with each name.

"All of them, all those six people dancing out there. There's my mom with the glitter in her hair. Then there's Dad with the glitter in his beard. That's Pinkie who's laughing and Douglas who has on the Count Dracula tux. It's his grandfather's and was new in 1928. I think he got it in Transylvania. That's a joke. Out west is where he got it, I think. And, there's my friend, The Wrench, dancing-pushing Mrs. Warren."

"Thank you, dear boy, you are very lucky to have such a big family. I only have a husband, who's dead, and a daughter, who may be, I can't remember. I hope she's not. I certainly do."

"I hope not too." Andrew puts down his light and asks Mrs. Herbert to dance. She puts her teeth in and they do a little in-place boogie to the old rock medley Ozone had fished out of her cabinet and brought up to the party. Her girlhood favs, I gather. Something about a pink carnation, a teen angel. Later, Richie says he knew the music from *Peggy Sue Got Married.*

The punch and cookies and dancing make the canned dinner taste good. The six of us—Andrew's family—and two aides from the kitchen are able to get everyone's tray ready. Richie helps Mrs. Green and I see her, though I can't hear, say a few more words to him. Later he tells me she was saying her poem again. After dinner I help the night shift get people ready for bed while Pinkie and Douglas and Rich and Andrew and Richie and The Wrench clean up the sparkle and turned-over trays. They mop up the grape juice we had spilled. Mrs. Osborne says the decorations can stay up until the twenty-sixth.

"Five days, wow, but at least I got extra credit for this with Ms. Sowers. I wish she could have stayed for the dance and supper."

Andrew's spiked hair is not drooping but his eyes have shadows. He is beginning to look tired.

"It's getting late, for Elder Home, near eight-thirty." I sound like an upbeat, in-charge administrative assistant. "Ask Ms. Woods and Ms. Sowers to come for dinner, then," suggests Richie, not even looking at me. "They could come when Officer Armentrout comes over to tell us about the prison talent show and The Wrench's mom comes over to hear what she missed tonight. There would be plenty to talk about. I am sure Ms. Vincent could come."

"Good thinking," Douglas says walking toward us. "Pinkie and Rich said for me to say they will see us soon, at the farm, they hope. Maybe we can get a smaller tree for the apartment tomorrow. They had to hurry. Hungry horses, I think."

The boys get in the car, Home sits in the front with me. Andrew and The Wrench get her seat belt buckled around her, then get in the back. Behind us, Douglas drives his car. Richie sits beside him, looking pleased.

About the Author

SUSAN PEPPER ROBBINS grew up in Cumberland County, Virginia, where she now lives with her husband and two sons. She teaches at Hampden-Sydney College.

About the Type

This book was set in Caledonia, a typeface designed in 1939 by William Addison Dwiggins for the Merganthaler Linotype Company. Its name is the ancient Roman term for Scotland, because the face was intended to have a Scotch-Roman flavor. Caledonia is considered to be a well-proportioned, businesslike face with little contrast between its thick and thin lines.